"I'm just trying to do the job I was hired to do here," Alison said softly

"And I'm just trying to live my life here," Mitch told her.

"Part of your life is in Dependable, Missouri."

"No, it's not."

She grabbed his arm. "You owe it to Joseph McCoy to say that to his face."

The desperation in her touch was hard to ignore. He did it anyway. "I don't owe him a thing, Miss Sullivan."

She mimicked his stance. "Is that a fact."

His hand slipped from the back door, and she let go of him. "If you don't come back with me, he'll just send someone else. You can't make it go away."

Icy determination poured into his veins. "That's where you're wrong, Alison. I know exactly how to make it go away...."

Dear Reader,

I can't think of anything as romantic as a cowboy.

Okay, I can, but that's because it's my job. Still, the idea of being swept off my feet by a man as strong and independent as the land he's dedicated his life to is my favorite fantasy. Or at least one of them. Clearly, I am well suited to the career I've been blessed with!

And what a perfect kind of hero to make life interesting for all the powerful McCoys in the second installment of my LOST MILLIONAIRES series.

Nothing about Mitch Smith—other than his mere existence, that is—would threaten the morally upright (despite his billions) reputation of the McCoy family patriarch, Joseph McCoy, but Mitch's stubbornness would threaten the patience of a saint.

Alison Sullivan is no saint, but she's a woman with her whole future hanging by a thread. Being hired to bring one of the illegitimate McCoy heirs into the fold is her salvation. And as stubborn as any cowboy might be, he's no match for a gal from Dependable, Missouri.

Enjoy the fireworks!

Leah Vale

P.S. I love to hear from readers. You can write to me at www.leahvale.com.

THE COWBOY
Leah Vale

HARLEQUIN®

TORONTO • NEW YORK • LONDON
AMSTERDAM • PARIS • SYDNEY • HAMBURG
STOCKHOLM • ATHENS • TOKYO • MILAN • MADRID
PRAGUE • WARSAW • BUDAPEST • AUCKLAND

ISBN 0-373-75038-2

THE COWBOY

Copyright © 2004 by Leah Vroman.

www.eHarlequin.com

Printed in U.S.A.

For Dad.
Because he likes the ones with the dogs in them.

Chapter One

Dear Mr. Smith,

It is our duty at this time to inform you of the death of Marcus McCoy due to an unfortunate, unforeseen encounter with a grizzly bear while fly-fishing in Alaska on June 8 of this year, and per the stipulations set forth in his last will and testament, to make formal his acknowledgment of one Mitchell Davis Smith, aka Mitch Smith, age 31, of the Circle S Ranch, Rural Route 5, Whiskey Ridge, Colorado, as being his son and heir to an equal portion of his estate.

It is the wish of Joseph McCoy, father to Marcus McCoy, grandfather to Mitch Smith, and founder of McCoy Enterprises, that you immediately assume your rightful place in the family home and business with all due haste and utmost discretion to preserve the family's privacy.

Regards,

David Weidman, Esq.

Weidman, Biddermier, Stark

Mitch squinted at the letter in his hand, the June Colorado morning sun reflecting brightly off the expensive white business stationery. He laid his dusty work gloves over the top rail of the corral and tipped his tan cowboy hat back with his finger. His squint deepened into a frown as he tuned out the bawling Angus calves behind him. Even after a second reading, the letter still made no sense, and the day wasn't even that hot yet.

He settled his forearms on the rail and looked up at the leggy redhead who'd brought his men to a standstill in the middle of inoculating some prize calves. She'd sashayed from her rented white pickup truck in high-heeled black boots, snug black jeans and a black knit top to hand-deliver the envelope bearing this letter to him.

It wasn't every day that a woman who looked like a darker-haired Nicole Kidman in one of his crews' favorite movies, *Days of Thunder,* showed up in U-Haul Rental pickups. He could tell from the conspicuous lack of whistles and shouts behind him that she still had their interest.

He nodded at the letter. "What *is* this?"

"Just what it says." Her voice had a rasp to it, as if she'd had a little too much fun the night before. Which might explain her lack of anything bordering on friendliness. He certainly knew the type. And did his damnedest to steer clear of them after almost committing himself to one. He wouldn't have had a dime to his name within a year.

He waited for more explanation, staring at a distorted

reflection of himself in her dark, rimless sunglasses. Didn't get any.

Great. A tight-lipped female when he wanted answers. So far all she'd done was ask if he was the Mitch Smith who owned this ranch, then handed him an envelope with a ringless left hand.

"Well, Miss…?"

She hesitated a moment, shifting her weight to one scary pointy-toed boot, then supplied, "Sullivan. Alison Sullivan."

"Well, Miss Sullivan, what I think this is, is a mistake. I've heard of the McCoys—at least the ones who own all those stores that sell just about everything. Are we talking about the same McCoys?"

At her emphatic nod, he shook his head. "Then I sure as hell have never met one. Or know anyone who has. Sorry, but you've got the wrong man." He folded the letter up and tucked it into the envelope.

When he handed it back to her, she just stared at it, her lips—much fuller than Miss Kidman's, he realized now that he really looked at her—parting slightly.

She shook her head with conviction. "No. There's no mistake." She yanked off her sunglasses and pinned him to the rail with the prettiest blue-green eyes he'd ever seen. "The McCoys hired me—my private investigation firm—to find you, Mitchell Davis Smith, deliver this letter, then escort you to Dependable, Missouri."

She took the letter back out of the envelope and thrust it at him.

Mitch had no choice but to take it. "Ah. That explains the bad-to-the-bone look." He shrugged and straightened away from the corral fence. "Then there must be another Mitchell Davis Smith running around somewhere, because I think I would have known if my natural father had been—" he glanced down at the letter "—Marcus McCoy. Him being a member of one of the richest families in the states, and all."

She took a step closer to the rail and placed her hand where his forearms had been, lending an air of intimacy to their conversation that would catch any man's interest. She glanced at the three men behind him and leaned forward more. Not that Carl, Juan or Richie could hear her over the noise of calves unhappy about being separated from their mamas.

In a low voice she said, "No, you wouldn't have. Your mother was paid a million dollars to keep your true paternity a secret."

Mitch froze.

A million dollars.

Mitch, we're so proud of the man you've become. It's time for you to have the money I received when your real father died.

What had started out as a million dollars before taxes had been sitting in an account since before he'd been born. The interest it piled up had been more than enough for the down payment on his maternal great-grandfather's old ranch. The ranch he'd yearned to bring back into the family since his mother first lulled him to sleep as a kid with stories of her visits here when she'd been a child.

He wiped away the echo of his mother's words along with the sweat on his brow. "No," he insisted to the gorgeous P.I., as well as to the spark of doubt that flared in his chest. "My mom's first husband, my real father, died before I was born."

She nodded as if he'd just told her his cattle were the other white meat. "And you know this how?"

His hackles rose. "For your information, when the man I'd thought was my dad, Ed Smith, was diagnosed with heart disease around the time I first started college, my mom admitted that Ed wasn't my biological father. She was afraid I would worry about having inherited his health issues."

"And she hadn't told you before because...?"

Mitch raised his hands sharply at her insinuation. "Why in the heck am I telling you this?" Reining in his temper, he spread his hands wide. "Look, lady. You made a mistake. It happens. It's okay, I won't tell anyone. But as you can see—" he swept the hand holding the letter toward the corral filled with more than two dozen calves and the three men behind him "—I'm busy, so goodbye." Mitch turned to walk away.

"Your mother's name is Bonnie Larsen, and she's lived in Boulder all her life."

Her accurate statement stopped him in his tracks and made his heart skip a beat.

"Before she married Edward Smith—her only recorded marriage, by the way—she worked for a development firm that did business with McCoy Enterprises. Which was how she met, and apparently became involved with, one Marcus McCoy."

Shock, disbelief, disappointment—a whole riot of emotions—attacked him. Just as when he'd found out Ed wasn't really his dad, that Michelle and Megan weren't his full-blood sisters. Afraid of what might show in his eyes, Mitch was unwilling to meet Alison Sullivan, Private Investigator Extraordinaire's blue-green gaze. He changed course and ducked through the round corral rails next to her. He'd put this whole thing to rest once and for all.

She said, "You are his son, and have been acknowledged as such in his will. Per the stipulations of that will, I need you to accompany me to Missouri."

Mitch ignored her and headed across the dusty expanse jokingly referred to as the yard separating the house from the corral.

"Mr. Smith?" she called after him.

He lengthened his stride, his stomach churning and his heart pounding.

"Mr. Smith!"

Mitch jumped over the two stairs up to the low porch that circled his entire house, the heels of his cowboy boots sharp on the already-weathered new planking, and yanked open the screen and front doors.

He went inside, letting the screen door bang in his wake. The sound echoed through the empty house like a truck backfire. Going straight for the phone on the foyer wall across from the stairs, he punched in his mother's number.

"Mr. Smith, please—"

He turned toward the P.I. standing on the other side of the screen door and threw her a hard glare. The sight of him on the phone had her pressing her plump lips together in obvious frustration.

Welcome to the club, sister. If there was more to the story of his parentage than what had already been kept from him, he'd strangle his dear mother.

"Hello?" his mom answered in her usual cheery tone.

He skipped any preamble and got right to the matter at hand. "Mom, I've a lady P.I. standing here telling me that my real father was none other than Marcus McCoy, of the billionaire McCoys."

"What?"

Relief washed through Mitch. One colossal surprise in a guy's life was enough. But he still slowly asked the question so there would be no doubt. "Mom, was my biological father Marcus McCoy?"

His mom sputtered. "A P.I.? Do you know who hired her?"

The flood of reassurance ebbed. "The McCoys. Or at least their lawyers." He glanced down at the letter, smudged from the dirt that always managed to work its way through his leather gloves. "I guess this Marcus guy was killed, by a grizzly bear in Alaska, no less, and when they read his will, he claimed a Mitchell Davis Smith as his son and heir. I told her she had the wrong—"

"Oh, my Lord. Oh, my Lord," his mom chanted, rocketing his heart rate back up.

"Mom?"

"Oh, Mitch…"

"Mom!"

"Oh, honey…"

At that moment, he knew. The lady P.I. had been telling the truth.

Staggered by the height of the stack of lies his life had been built on, Mitch fisted the hand holding the letter and planted it on the wall above his head to steady himself.

His throat rapidly closing from the stranglehold being the last to know something so critical to his life for the second time, all he could force out was "Tell me."

ALISON STARED AT MITCHELL Davis Smith's broad back. His sweat-dampened light blue work shirt clung to every rise and crevice of his well-developed muscles. As he spoke to his mother on the phone with his tan cowboy hat askew, she held her breath.

Totally pointless, because she couldn't breathe, anyway. Her fingernails made it through the first layer of white paint on the frame of the two-story, prairie-Victorian-style house's front door as she gripped it for dear life. Also pointless, because no matter how hard she held on, she could feel her life spinning out of her control once again.

Something she'd sworn to never let happen.

But if she couldn't convince this gorgeous *Lonesome*

Dove refugee in dusty, form-fitting denim to accompany her back to Dependable, she wouldn't get paid the huge chunk of change promised to her, let alone the massive bonus for getting him there in time for Joseph McCoy's seventy-fifth birthday bash. She squeezed the door frame harder until she hit raw wood and willed the big man who'd taken her by surprise in more ways than one to accept the truth.

Assuming his mother was actually finally telling it to him.

Her oxygen-starved brain couldn't come up with a plan to counter his mother's possible refusal to come clean. The best she could do to get the Lost Millionaire she'd been sent to retrieve—one of three—to come with her was refuse to leave without him.

Those wide, stiff shoulders suddenly slumped and he cocked one knee, raising the hand holding the letter to the wall to hold his weight.

She felt a tiny spurt of hope. Alison bit down hard on her lower lip and waited.

He listened silently, the rise and fall of his chest increasing in tempo.

She felt a twinge of sympathy in her own chest, but as harsh at it might sound, his pain would be her gain.

Assuming he believed his mother.

Mitch Smith slammed the phone down hard onto its cradle and pulled Alison from the brink of her very first panic attack.

She dragged in a sanity-restoring breath, such as it

was on Colorado's high plains, an unbelievable mile above sea level. "She told you I'm right, didn't she?"

He dropped his chin to his chest and didn't answer.

A greater surge of empathy took advantage of the hole panic had blasted through her defenses and nailed her square in the heart. No. She would not feel sorry for this guy. He was a McCoy, for heaven's sake! What she wouldn't give for just a sliver of the money, *the security,* he had coming to him.

Her voice was nonetheless gentle when she added, "As surprises go, this one isn't all that bad, you know."

He exploded into action, pushing off the wall. Without looking at her, he headed into a room to the right of the front door.

"Mr. Smith?"

The thunk of his boot heels on the hardwood floor halted as he stopped somewhere out of her sight.

"Mr. Smith, may I please come in?"

She held her breath again. The silence inside the house stretched. Alison grabbed the screen door handle, then hesitated. She hadn't been invited in. While she was only ankle deep in her little dip into the private investigator job pool after her failed stint as Suzie homemaker, she figured entering a subject's home uninvited was probably a no-no.

And who knew what code of the Old West she might be breaking. From the look of Mr. Smith, with his dust-colored, sweat-stained cowboy hat and his beat-up brown cowboy boots, he clearly took this rancher thing seriously. There were no modern co-ops involved in his operation.

She moved to the side of the screen door and tried to see the room he'd disappeared into, but the partially open door blocked her view. She hurried to the closest of the two windows on that side of the door and slipped behind one of four oversize ladder-back rockers occupying the wraparound porch.

The sash on the window was pushed completely up, and she could see him standing in front of the empty fireplace in what looked to be the living room, but was so small it resembled an old-fashioned parlor room. Only, the furnishings weren't frilly or delicate or remotely Victorian.

A dark brown leather love seat faced the fireplace along with a matching oversize recliner. Snuggled up to each piece were reading lamps, clearly needed judging by the stacks of books and magazines on the old steamer trunk-turned-coffee table. A pair of polished steer horns hung on the wall.

Very much a man's room. She knew he wasn't married, but apparently there wasn't a woman close enough to him to be allowed much decorating input.

He'd braced his hands on the white carved mantel as he stared at a framed photo there. The glare from the window on the picture glass kept her from seeing the image.

Another twist of sympathy made her wince. She knew what it felt like to be blindsided. At least his little surprise could ultimately be considered a very good thing.

Alison bent to speak through the window screen. "Mr. Smith, we still have some matters to discuss."

"Such as?" he answered without looking at her, but his tone made it clear he didn't agree.

"When you'll be ready to accompany me to Dependable, Missouri, to see Joseph McCoy, for one. He's very anxious to meet you."

Mr. Smith grunted and pushed off the mantel, then strode away from her through a doorway on the far wall. Because of her angle, she could see a window like the one she was looking through in the room, so she sidled past the rocking chair and hurried around the corner, her high-heeled boots tapping loudly on the wraparound porch. She screeched to a halt and found herself looking into a large den.

The file cabinets and endless shelves holding books and row after row of thick black binders made it obvious that this was where he ran his burgeoning ranching operation. The equally masculine room looked tidy and well organized, a far cry from the way her ex-husband Scott had kept his office.

The cowboy planted one fist on the top of an open rolltop desk as he stood flipping through some papers so quickly he couldn't possibly be reading anything. The letter from the McCoy lawyers had been tossed on the desk alongside the papers. With a noise loaded with frustration and hurt, he swept the papers from the desk and sent them scattering across the floor.

He exhaled loudly and pulled his hat from his head

so he could run a hand through the thick, waving mass beneath, staring dolefully at the mess he'd made.

Alison stared at his hair, momentarily distracted. Even sweat-darkened, Mitch Smith's hair clearly wasn't the same jet-black color as the rest of the McCoy family's, though Joseph McCoy's had long since turned steely.

Mitch was a blond.

What if she *did* have the wrong man?

No. She shook off the momentary flash of doubt. Those piercing blue eyes and square jaw of his were classic McCoy. And the trail she'd followed through his mother's records had led right to Mitch's doorstep. Alison might be new at this, but she wasn't stupid. Scott and her father, in his overprotective—and ultimately chauvinistic—way, had made her doubt a lot of things, but never her intelligence.

The den window had been left open, also—whatever breeze might blow through apparently was worth the dust that would accompany it—so Alison bent to talk through the screen. "Mr. Smith—"

He turned toward her with a jerk, clearly startled. "I'd thought you'd taken the hint and left."

"Not until we discuss the arrangements that need to be made."

He slammed his hat back on his head. "I'm not discussing anything with you, lady." He stormed out of the den through a different door.

Alison grumbled and ran around the porch to the

back of the nicely maintained old house. A screened door as well as several windows faced the backyard, which looked suspiciously like the front, only the large corral back here was full of horses of all colors, not baby black cows. There were also a couple of barns off to the west side with the Rocky Mountains smudging the horizon beyond.

A hot tub had been added off the far edge of the porch. She could just imagine staring off at the distant snow-topped mountains while soaking in bubbling heat. Getting this guy to leave here was not going to be easy.

After skirting a covered barbecue grill, she headed for the screen door keeping the flies at bay while the white back door stood open, but she stopped short. On the doormat lay a mound of black, white and light brown fur. The mound surprisingly hadn't stirred at her noisy approach, but the long, thick fur rhythmically rose and fell. Being a firm believer in letting sleeping dogs lie or lay or whatever in the heck it was, she didn't move any closer.

Through the screen door she spotted her quarry. He was standing at the sink on the right side of the kitchen, splashing water on his face. His hat rested on the white tile counter next to him. His shirt stretched over an impossibly broad back.

Alison's gaze inadvertently traveled over the jeans-clad curve of his muscular rear end and thigh as he stood with one knee cocked. Her mouth went dry.

Dehydration, that was all. Despite having downed

what seemed like a case of bottled water on the way out here. She'd read up on how to stay in peak shape in the higher altitudes found in Colorado, and drinking plenty of water was one of the ways.

Like she'd ever be able to bodily haul Mitch Smith back to Dependable, peak shape or not. He had to be at least six-two, well over a head taller than her even in her boots. She needed his cooperation.

Keeping an eye on the multicolored fluff that surely had teeth somewhere even if it was deaf, she quietly made her way on tiptoe past the door and around the corner of the house to the window directly above the sink.

That window, too, had been opened all the way. While the appliances, and everything else for that matter, in the kitchen looked new, there clearly was no air-conditioning to be had in the place.

She waited to speak again until he hit the faucet handle with his forearm to turn off the water. "You must have questions that I might be able to answer."

He froze in the act of reaching for a white dish towel and raised his gaze to hers. His intense blue eyes glittered as much as the drops of water rolling down his chiseled face. His handsomeness sucked what little air there was right out of her lungs.

"The only thing I want to know is why you're still here."

"Because I can't leave without you."

"You expect me to drop everything and skip off with

you to Missouri the very day I find out I've been lied to by my own mother?"

The hurt and betrayal glowing in his gorgeous eyes and thickening his voice smacked into her like a city bus come out of nowhere and flattened any satisfaction she might have experienced from being right. Why had she allowed herself to come all the way out here so unprepared?

Oh, sure, she'd read every *Private Investigating for Idiots* type of book she could get her hands on. But she hadn't done a thing to mentally prepare herself for the impact the news she was delivering would have on her subject, let alone the impact of the man himself on *her.*

She cleared her throat, horribly aware of the inappropriateness of her empathy for him. "Yes. I mean, no, not necessarily today. But…but at least within the next couple of weeks. And definitely before the first week in July." To avoid bankruptcy she *had* to get that bonus she'd receive for having this Lost Millionaire in Dependable for Joseph McCoy's birthday party on July 3. "Once we decide on a date, I can leave. If you don't want to go right away, I can always go home, then fly back to accompany you."

But she knew what Joseph really hoped for was that she return with this particular grandson in tow as soon as possible.

With slow purpose, he grabbed the dish towel from the counter and dried his face. Alison's nerves stretched taut with each passing second.

He finally looked at her. "Miss...Sullivan, was it?"

She nodded, torn between eagerness and dread.

"Miss Sullivan, not only will I not be accompanying you to Dependable, Missouri, today or any other day, but I want you off my ranch."

Alison immediately opened her mouth to protest. "I—"

He lowered his chin and the bitter product of his mother's betrayal became plain on his face. "Now."

Chapter Two

Alison took an involuntary step back at the unquestionable authority in his voice. But her situation didn't allow for the luxury of cowering. Or giving up.

She swallowed her fear of confrontation and baldly stated, "I can't. Not without you. Or at least your sworn agreement to accompany me later."

He threw down the dish towel and headed for the back door. She heard him grumble "Look out, Hoss," before the squeak and slam of the screen door. The sharp rap of his boots on the porch heralded his approach a second before he rounded the corner of the house.

She'd never seen a man so resemble a charging bull in her life. And despite her no-nonsense, noir monochromatic look, he was definitely seeing red.

It took every scrap of courage she had to hold her ground. To keep that fact from showing, she crossed her arms over her chest and threw out a Missouri hip.

His pace didn't slow as he reached her, but he snagged

her elbow and pronounced, "You can, and you will," as he pulled her backward with him.

Her new stiletto boots weren't easy to walk forward in, let alone while being hauled backward, so it took her a moment of forced concentration to keep from landing on her rear before she could protest.

"Mr. Smith! There's no call for this sort of manhandling!" While his grip on her elbow was strong, he wasn't actually hurting her. But he didn't need to know that.

He came to an abrupt stop. "Am I hurting you?"

The challenge in his tone and the determination in his bright blue gaze, rather than concern, had her blurting, "Yes!" even though he was only hurting her pride.

"My apologies," he offered, with zero sincerity. He let go of her elbow but promptly reached across her to grab her other one and turned her so she faced forward. His grip not much lighter and a whole lot more disconcerting, he started hauling her toward the front of the house again.

She opted not to try to dig the high, thin heels of her boots in since she'd probably only break one off, or an ankle, or her neck on the wooden porch.

He led her toward the stairs, cautioning "Mind your step," with ridiculous politeness, considering the fact he was dragging her from his porch like the garbage.

Hysterical laughter welled up right along with the return of a hearty dose of panic. In a desperate attempt to cling to her newfound professionalism, she grit her teeth, only to end up jarring her molars when his pace forced her to jump past the last step to the hard-packed ground.

His men stopped what they were doing to watch the spectacle.

Embarrassment stung in her cheeks. Enough was enough. "Mr. Smith! I insist you allow me to speak with you about this." She pulled back against his hold on her elbow, locked her knees and set her weight on her heels.

His attention still on her rental truck and his grip tightening only slightly, he pulled her along as if she weighed nothing. Her heels dug furrows in the dirt and created a dust cloud in her wake. When he reached the white pickup with the rental company's logo emblazoned along its entire length, he yanked open the driver's door.

He stunned her even further by scooping her up in his arms and plopping her on the seat.

Alison blinked against the fleeting impression of strength, heat and a smell far too pleasant considering what the man had been doing when she'd arrived. He topped off his performance by slamming the door shut.

Wishing it could be his neck, she grabbed hold of the steering wheel, squeezing until her knuckles turned white. She met his glare through the open window. "My, but that was an impressive show of caveman-itis."

"Goodbye, Miss Sullivan. Give the McCoys my regrets." He turned and started walking back toward the corral, where even the calves had stopped their complaining to join the three other cowboys in watching her humiliation.

She wrung the very life from the hot black steering wheel. She yelled, "I'm not going to leave, you know. I'm going to sit here until you agree to come with me. And if you don't, well, I'm sure you'll barely notice the stink from my carcass over the smell of those cows. Though the ruckus the buzzards will make might get on your nerves. Oh, and the rental company will probably start bugging you about the truck." She reached a hand through the window and loudly patted the outside of the driver's door. "Eventually."

He stopped, and she could see the chest that had turned out to be as hard as it looked expand as he inhaled slowly. Turning on his boot heel, he marched back toward her, his square jaw set. "Fine." He jerked the driver's door open again. "Scoot. I'm driving."

She was too surprised to do more than gape at him, and he had to push her across the bench seat with his hip and shoulder as he climbed behind the wheel. His big body consumed the cab and made her extremely aware of her femininity, but her stupid reaction to him didn't matter because she'd won. He was coming with her. She'd done it!

He shut the door with enough force to rattle the frame, started the truck and slammed it into gear.

Alison hoped that his anger would last long enough to put some miles behind them on the way to the Denver airport. Eventually he'd cool off enough to realize he didn't have any other clothes or toiletries. She'd gladly buy whatever he needed out of her own pocket to get this job done. Her whole world depended on a successful completion.

So she kept quiet as he barreled down the dusty drive to the gravel road that would take them out to the two-lane road leading to Whiskey Ridge, then on to Ault and the main highway.

They only got as far as the beginning of the gravel road before he slammed on the brakes, sending bits of rock flying into the truck's wheel wells with loud pings. Her big black satchel was tossed to the floorboard from where it had been pushed along the seat next to her. Alison reflexively braced her hands on the red dashboard above the glove compartment.

Jamming the gearshift into Park, he bailed out and left her staring after him, slack-jawed.

He stomped toward a big metal gate that had been left open and that she frankly hadn't even noticed when she'd driven in.

Relief washed over her. He was simply closing the gate on their way out. She twisted to watch him through the truck's back window.

He tugged on the gate several times before he could get it to move, then guided the obviously heavy gate as it swung closed...*from the inside, not the side she and the truck were on.* She held her breath as he secured the latch on the gate, then threaded a heavy metal chain wrapped around the thick post through the gate and locked it with a huge padlock.

Willing him to climb through or over the gate, Alison flattened a hand against the window a second before he tipped his hat at her, turned and sauntered away.

He'd neatly outsmarted her.

No, he hadn't. He'd simply used his physical superiority to bully her off his property.

She fisted her hand and smacked it against the window.

The temptation to leap from the truck, climb over the gate and chase him down roared through her. But he'd probably call the sheriff and have her arrested for trespassing. And she didn't have the money to spare for a fine or bail.

Alison rubbed at her temples, trying to calm down. She needed to be rational. She needed to think.

Okay, so he'd won this round.

He was sadly mistaken if he thought she'd give up now, though. The memory of Scott's mocking laughter flooded her with determination liberally spiked with anger. Maybe being calm was overrated. She sure as heck knew being passive was.

She slid across the bench seat to behind the truck's steering wheel and reached for the door Mitch had left open. She slammed it closed hard, resisting the temptation to look in the rearview mirror to see if he'd turned at the noise. He probably hadn't, which would just steam her more.

Despite what Mitchell Davis Smith might think, this wasn't over. And there was more than one way to shanghai a cowboy.

ON HIS WAY INTO TOWN, Mitch had to look twice at the white U-Haul rental parked off to the side of the road before he could believe what he was seeing as he drove by. He'd been thinking about the blasted woman with her endless legs and beautiful but panic-tinged blue-green eyes so much in the last three days that he halfway thought he was imagining things.

But there was no mistaking the high-heeled black boots propped up on the dashboard among all sorts of paper cups and food wrappers. He looked in his rear-view mirror just in time to see the boots jerk down and a dark red head pop up. Dust flew as the truck peeled out to follow him.

Apparently Alison Sullivan hadn't given up as he'd thought.

His heart rate picked up as he alternated his attention between the two-lane highway in front of him and the truck pulling up close behind him. He told himself he was just annoyed. Nothing to do with the fact that in the middle of the night he'd momentarily wished he'd met her in a different way, in a different time in his life. And it had to do with more than just her looks. He'd admired her spunk.

Now, not so much.

He could see her behind the wheel, with her dark sun-glasses and mane of red hair blowing around in the wind from the open windows. Her rental truck must not have working air-conditioning. An unpleasant prospect

as they headed into summer. She had to be seriously tenacious or seriously desperate to be sitting out there
waiting for him to poke his head off his property. Something he'd been known not to do for weeks at a time
when he was busy.

Lucky for her he had to pick up an order at the hardware store and grab a few groceries today.

Not that following him into town would do her any
good other than give her a chance to cool off. Physically,
at least. He had every intention of ignoring her as he
went about his business. He'd show her stubborn.

His mom had known better than to try calling him
back more than once after she'd tossed him the second
bomb of his life. He hadn't answered then because there
wasn't much else she could say to him. The whys and
wherefores didn't matter now.

All that mattered was his land. The one thing in his
life he could trust without question.

Miss Sullivan stuck as close to his white dually as she
dared the whole way into town. While he knew it was
childish, the devil in him had him flooring the accelerator, then braking at random intervals to make the trip
interesting. When he pulled into one of the angled parking spots on the main drag in front of Whiskey Ridge
Hardware and Farm Supplies, she pulled into the space
next to him, undeterred.

He climbed out of his truck and headed for the store's
door as if he hadn't noticed her or the fact that she was
hustling out of her truck to catch him. Or that she had

on a snug, short-sleeved black T-shirt and blue jeans with her spike-heeled black boots. Nothing extraordinary, but her slender beauty somehow made the look very urban casual. And very hard to ignore.

From behind him she said, "I think you should have your fuel-intake valve looked at, Mr. Smith. Your rig seems to be running a little irregularly."

His step faltered. Her sly wit was unexpected, but he still didn't acknowledge her as he reached the door and pushed it open.

The bell jingled over his head and prompted his habitual greeting of "Hey, Harv," coupled with a tug on the brim of his cowboy hat.

Harvey Appleton glanced up from the sales slip he was writing out for one of Mitch's neighbors, Ben Jennings, at the long counter next to the door. His thick sandy brows unfurrowed and his round face crinkled all over as he smiled the trademark smile that had been greeting the folks of Whiskey Ridge for forty-odd years. "Hey, Mitch."

At the same time, Ben pulled on the bill of the green John Deere baseball cap he claimed with a straight face he always wore because it matched his eyes. As Ben was more the dry-humor sort, his smile was more subdued. "Mitch."

"Morning, Ben."

Harvey held up the stub of a pencil he was using. "Just a second and I'll get your ord—"

The bell jingled again.

The absence of any "Hey, Harv," and Harvey and Ben's slack-jawed expression, let Mitch know exactly who had come in behind him, and she wasn't local.

Though they were both happily married, as far as Mitch knew, Ben stood up straighter to lessen the excess red plaid hanging over his belt and Harvey smoothed hair that was no longer there.

Acting as if his other two customers didn't exist, Harvey eagerly offered, "May I help you find anything, miss?"

The pretty P.I. with a stubborn slant to her auburn brows instantly transformed into a heartbreaking beauty when she flashed Harvey a killer smile. "Why, thank you for the offer, but I'm just here with him." She nodded toward Mitch.

Mitch scowled at her and opened his mouth to say like hell she was, but Harvey's brows shot up and he exclaimed, "Mitch! Where in heaven's name did you hook up with a looker like her? Let alone find the time?"

Mitch sputtered, "We're not—"

"On the Internet," Little Miss Tenacious blithely tossed out, then directed a smug smile at Mitch. "We met in a chat room."

Ben whispered plenty loud, "Oh, boy. I know somebody who's not gonna like that."

Mitch silently groaned and had time to see her smile slip before he turned toward the nearest aisle stacked high with just about everything a working ranch might need. "She's not with me," he declared as he stalked away.

He heard Miss Sullivan say in a conspiratorial tone,

"I didn't warn him that I was coming to visit, so he didn't have a chance to straighten up his place. He's a little miffed."

Miffed? Good thing his mother had been better at raising a gentleman than she'd been at telling the truth, or he'd show Miss Sullivan how seriously *crapped off* he really was.

Toward the other end of the aisle he snatched up a box of crankcase oil. With the box held out in front of him, he wheeled back around only to find her standing right in front of him. How in the world did she move so fast in those stilts masquerading as boots?

He forced himself to ignore the way her blue-green eyes glowed with determination. "What the hell—"

She hissed, "I was hired to do this with the utmost discretion, Mr. Smith."

Rolling his eyes, he retorted, "Oh, yeah, and claiming to be my Internet score in a small town like Whiskey Ridge is the way to keep things hush-hush."

Though he had to admit, her cock-and-bull story was far better than the truth. No one around here even knew about the first lie he'd been told. The fact that Ed wasn't his real father had been kept between his family and their doctors.

"Mr. Smith." She stepped close enough that he could smell her. A woman who'd been camped out in a rental truck without air-conditioning should not smell so damn good. Like a meadow of wildflowers after it rained.

"Mitch," he absently corrected.

Her expression softened and she shifted closer still. The smooth cotton of her black T-shirt brushed against his knuckles as he held the box of oil out in front of him. The contact drew his attention to her breasts—not real big, but full—molded beneath the snug fabric, and tapped directly into his otherwise easily controlled libido.

"All I'm asking for is just a little help with this, *Mitch.*" Her tone was conciliatory with a side order of sexual temptation. His body was instantly up for extra helpings.

Out of the corner of his eye he saw Harvey and Ben wander all casual-like past the aisle, looking his way until they disappeared. Their curiosity was enough to snap him out of whatever spell her mesmerizing eyes and scent had put him under.

He jerked back a step and bumped his elbow against a row of spray lubricant, knocking over several cans with a clatter. Harvey and Ben reappeared at the end of the aisle like a couple of dogs who'd heard their dish rattle. Mitch clenched his back teeth at the mess this whole thing was becoming and tucked the box under his arm.

He stepped back toward her, leaning close so only she would hear him and ruthlessly ignoring her enticing scent. "I thought I made my feelings pretty clear when I tossed you off my ranch, Miss Sullivan."

She frowned and opened her mouth.

He moved past her. "It was nice meeting you. Have a safe trip back home," he said as he headed toward the front of the store and the two men trying to look as if they were extremely interested in the penny-nail bins.

A decidedly feminine grumbling sounded behind Mitch, and this time he could hear her heels on the linoleum flooring as she followed him.

He mentally blocked the noise out. "Harv, do you have that clutch cable for me or not?"

"Oh, sure, Mitch. Right behind the counter." Harvey jumped into action, hustling to beat Mitch to the checkout counter. Ben slipped over to the work-glove display and studied it intensely, despite having a perfectly decent-looking pair hanging out of his jeans' back pocket.

Mitch could feel Miss Sullivan hovering behind him while he paid for the case of crankcase oil and the clutch cable he needed for one of his all-terrain vehicles. She stayed silent, but dogged his heels when he left the hardware store.

"The McCoys are an honorable family who at least deserve your acknowledgement, you know," she argued while he put the boxes into the back of his truck.

He set his jaw and ignored her. He'd get the coffee, juice and other groceries he needed, then hightail it back to the Circle S. Mitch crossed the street to Mabel's Market without a glance in either direction, knowing he'd hear any traffic coming a long way off.

The same was true of her heels on the pavement as she chased him.

She caught up with him at the curb. "Aren't you the slightest bit interested in the fact you have three half brothers?"

So much for ignoring her. While he hadn't checked

for traffic, he did check the sidewalk for nosy neighbors. No one was close, though Harvey and Ben were watching from the door of the hardware store.

He pulled his hat lower on his brow and headed for the door to the market. "Nope. Got two half sisters that do their share of annoying." It had taken him a few years, but he'd finally realized it wasn't so much shared genes that made Michelle and Megan his siblings, but shared experiences.

She stared at him as if he'd just mooed. "You don't want to meet them?"

"Nope." He opened the glass door covered with handwritten announcements of current sales and upcoming events such as the community festival this weekend.

He automatically held the door open for her, then thought, *doh!* The last thing he wanted was to encourage her to follow him around.

As she stepped past him, she asked, "Why?"

He followed her through the door, asking himself the same question, and was pleased to be able to tell her the truth. "I am just plain not interested."

"Well, your grandfather—" she glanced around "—Joseph McCoy, is certainly interested in *you.*"

Finally having caught a break in that no one was in sight, he strode past the unmanned cash register to the refrigerated section. Mabel must be stocking shelves or doing something in the storeroom.

"Well," he shot back, "I'm sorry to disappoint, but I

have a ranch to run." It was the only thing he could trust hands down anymore. He took out two jugs of orange juice and shut the glass door with his knee.

"I don't see what it would hurt to take a quick trip to Dependable with me." She trailed after him to the beverage aisle.

"Did you see those three guys in that corral with me the other day? Most of the time it's just them and me working the Circle S. Nearly ten thousand acres of it. While I'd put my life in Carl, Juan or Richie's hands in the blink of an eye, that ranch is mine. It's my responsibility."

Realizing too late that he hadn't grabbed a basket, he started to tuck one of the juice jugs under his arm so he could grab a can of coffee, but she took it from him. "Thanks. And I have no intention of dropping everything to run off to Missouri." He went to get the sugar.

"It's *Mizzura*."

He glanced back at her as he walked. Her forehead was bunched and her full mouth was turned down. "What?"

"We don't say *Missuree,* we say *Mizzura* in Dependable."

"You can say whatever you want. I don't care, and I'm not going."

Without being asked, she relieved him of the coffee so he could pick up a ten-pound bag of sugar. It was as if they'd been shopping together forever. He rolled his eyes at the thought and started for the checkout counter. Like she could ever be the helpmate he wanted.

Thankfully, she hung back and stayed quiet while he smacked the dinger to let Mabel know she was needed. She was a little hard of hearing, which seemed to be the only concession she'd made to turning seventy.

Mabel came through the storeroom door, wiping her hands on her ever-present flowered-and-ruffled pink apron that was such an odd contrast to her jeans, men's work shirt and tennis shoes. Her lined face lit up when she saw him and made him smile and wink at her despite his annoyance with the P.I.

"Mitch, dear! How are you?" She quickly patted her white hair.

"I'm great, Mabel," he lied, and set the jug of juice and bag of sugar down on the counter. Miss Sullivan slipped next to him and placed the jug she was carrying, along with the coffee, next to the other items.

Mabel's mouth dropped open. "Alison? Don't tell me Mitch is the friend you've been hoping to bump into? I told you I'd probably know whomever you were waiting on!"

Mitch glanced at the pretty P.I. who'd tried to skulk back behind him, thinking of the pile of food wrappers on the dash of her rental truck. While there was a decent-size Go-food on the corner coming into town from the west and all three of the gas stations sold food of some kind, she must have discovered that Mabel had by far the widest selection of just about everything for a heck of a lot less money.

With red tingeing the fair skin beneath her sculpted

cheekbones, she shrugged and gave Mabel a sheepish smile. "'Spose I should have told you."

Mabel forgave her with a wave and started ringing up Mitch's groceries and bagging them. "As long as you found him, which you clearly have. But a stud like him's hard to miss."

Loving Mabel's youthful exuberance, he teased, "Keep that up, Mabel, and you'll find me haunting your doorstep like one of your alley cats."

When he looked back at Miss Sullivan, he saw that the flush on her cheeks had brightened and spread down her neck. Not the cool cucumber she'd first portrayed at all. He could understand her heated reaction to his refusal to cooperate with her, but this embarrassment over Mabel's comments was interesting.

And completely irrelevant. Whether he should pity the messenger or not, he still wasn't responding to the royal summons.

Mabel asked Miss Sullivan, "So how do you know our Mitch?"

Mitch interjected, "Mabel, sweetheart, can you make change for a fifty?" He didn't want Miss Sullivan to add to the Internet rumor or spin a new yarn.

Successfully distracted, Mabel said, "Of course I can, hon."

Mitch pulled out his wallet and handed over the bill, then picked up one of the two brown bags and handed it to Miss Sullivan. "Could you put this on the floor in the cab of my truck? Thanks." He cupped her elbow and started her toward the door before she could protest.

Mabel turned back to him with his change just in time to see Miss Sullivan leave the store. "Oh."

Her disappointment over the younger woman's departure was obvious. Anything—but particularly anyone—new and different around here was always appreciated. He'd make it up to Mabel somehow later.

As was her style, she shrugged it off. "Well, she is just a doll. And pretty! So how did—"

He tilted his head and made a show of looking at her watch. "Wow, is that the time? Uh-oh." He raised his own bare arm before he snagged the last bag. "Don't wear one. Too easy to get caught up on something. Gotta go. Bye, Mabel."

"Bye, hon. Next time, buy some fresh veggies!" she called after him, but he was already hauling it out the door.

He shouldn't have hurried quite so much, though, because he reached his truck just in time to see Miss Sullivan bend over into the open passenger door to put the grocery bag inside.

Whoa, baby.

Yep, ignoring her was definitely out now.

She straightened and stepped aside so he could move past her. He stuck his head into the truck to put his own bag on the floorboard, and discovered she'd left more than the bag behind. Great, now his truck smelled like her. The lingering scent, coupled with the image of her firm little rear seared in his brain, made it tough to think.

"I'm just trying to do the job I was hired to do, here," she said softly behind him.

He ducked back out of the cab to face her, telling himself she wasn't all that pretty. "And I'm trying to live my life, here."

"Part of your life is in Dependable, Missouri."

Feeling a little bad for the glitter of desperation in her eyes, he slung a hand over the truck door and cocked a knee. "No, it's not."

She grabbed his arm. "You owe it to Joseph McCoy to say that to his face."

The desperation in her touch was harder to ignore. He did it anyway. "I don't owe him a thing, Miss Sullivan."

She mimicked his stance. "Is that a fact."

Your mother was paid a million dollars to keep your true paternity a secret.

The memory of her words hung between them, as if she'd spoken them again. His hand slipped from the truck door.

She let go of him. "If you don't come back with me, he'll just send someone else. You can't make it go away, Mitch."

Icy determination poured into his veins. "That's where you're wrong, Alison. I know exactly how to make it go away."

Chapter Three

Alison jumped back as Mitch slammed the truck's passenger door and stormed away. Panic swirled up from what was becoming its permanent spot in her stomach. Her stomach lining would be trashed for sure by the end of this ordeal.

Unfortunately, the end appeared to be coming way too soon.

The man with her future in his hands was stomping away from her, heading up the two-lane main street of his dinky little town like an indignant bulldog, and she had no choice but to chase after him yet again.

If only he would cooperate! Who in their right mind wouldn't want to be welcomed into the billionaire McCoy family? Maybe Mitch Smith didn't wear his hat all the time when out in the hot sun, after all, and had baked his brain at some point.

She hadn't quite caught up to him when he crossed the street, but she was tight on his boot heels by the time he entered another of the Old West-style stores that lined the street.

She had no idea what he was up to, but there was no way she could let him make this "go away."

It took a moment for Alison to realize that she'd followed him into a small bank, and the swirling panic spread until her fingers tingled and felt hot from it. Going off nothing but a sickening foreboding, she grabbed at the back of his tan work shirt just above his waistband. He continued to pretend she wasn't there and stepped up to the lone female teller standing behind a counter directly across from the entrance.

The attractive young blonde with a pouty pink mouth that matched her silk blouse looked up from a form she was filling out. Her brown eyes flared with recognition and appreciation of the man in front of her. She flipped her stick-straight long hair and flashed Mitch a provocative smile. "Hey, Mitch."

"Krissi."

The teller's gaze caught on Alison and her expression hardened. "Who's your friend?" There was nothing friendly about her tone.

Maybe she was the somebody the man in the hardware store knew who wouldn't be happy about Mitch meeting a woman online. Normally Alison would have felt guilty about her off-the-cuff lie, but she couldn't afford to feel guilty about anything that would help her get this job done.

Mitch rubbed the back of his neck.

Alison knew from the information she'd gathered on Mr. Mitchell Davis Smith that he'd never been married, but he could very well have a girlfriend. He was, after all, drop-dead gorgeous and worthy of the romanticism attached to honest-to-goodness cowboys.

She straightened her spine against the ridiculous disappointment tugging at her belly. Besides, it wasn't like he'd been earning any points with the old-fashioned charm these guys were supposed to ooze.

Mitch only gave Alison a glance before saying, "Is Donald in, by any chance?"

Fine. She *wasn't* his friend. And she was more than willing to be his worst nightmare if he didn't allow her to complete this job. Even if he did look a little green at the moment. She mentally pinched off the sprout of sympathy for him still trying to grow in her chest. Just because the man was positively stiff with pride, she sure didn't need to feel sorry for him because he'd been lied to all his life.

Long blond hair flicked again, only this time in irritation. "No. He's not."

Mitch pushed his hat farther back on his forehead, revealing the sweat-dampened hair at his temples. "Any chance he'll be in soon?"

Krissi's eyes darted between Alison and Mitch, the jealous speculation clear to see. "'Fraid not. He's in Denver on bank business." Her gaze on Mitch. Resting her elbows on the counter, she leaned forward. "Guess you'll just have to settle for me." The invitation to more than banking business was plain.

Oh, there was history here, all right. And Krissi either didn't consider Alison a threat or she was willing to fight for him.

Something Scott hadn't given Alison a chance to do. She waited for the old hurt to throb, and was glad when it only pricked in the vicinity of her own overabundant pride. She sure as heck hoped she didn't walk around looking like a bulldog, too.

Mitch glanced at Alison again and she realized she'd tightened her hold on the back of his shirt. She quickly released him and shifted away, crossing her arms over her chest. His gaze hot with frustration and something else she couldn't identify, he studied her for a moment longer before looking back at Krissi.

"I need my account balances, both personal and business, plus the financial planning papers that list my assets."

Alison blinked. Was he going to try to buy her off? As desperate as she was for cash, her need to prove herself capable of succeeding was greater. She had to prove Scott and her father wrong.

Krissi raised her brows at him before turning to her computer. "Oka-ay." She drew the word out. As she typed, she gave Alison another quick look. "What's up?"

He crossed his arms over his chest, too. "Nothing."

Her Kewpie-doll lips tightened and her long pink nail clicked when she hit the last key. A printer beneath the counter whirred. She retrieved the papers as they came out, tsking before she handed them to Mitch. "I told you that you could afford to take me to nicer restaurants." A glint in her eyes revealed the calculating woman beneath the sex-kitten facade.

Definitely some history. And not all good. Intriguing.

Mitch made a noise in the back of his throat and snatched the printouts from Krissi, confirming Alison's assumption about their past.

Krissi didn't seem to mind. "Those are your account balances. It'll take me a minute to get the other papers from Donald's files." She turned and went through a door off to the side of the counter.

The second she was gone, Alison demanded, "What's this all about?"

He didn't look up from the printouts. "I'm going to make this all go away."

Her mouth went dry. "How?"

In a low, gruff voice he said, "I'm going to cut all ties to the McCoys by paying back the million dollars they gave my mother for her silence. Even if I have to drain my bank accounts, sell off some assets and take out a second mortgage."

Alison's arm went limp and she fell back a step. "You can't."

He looked at her, his expression hard and grim. Only the shadow of pain darkening his blue eyes hinted at what his decision cost him. "I can, and I will." His voice sounded strangled but revealed the force of his will. "We've been operating in the black for the past two years, so—"

"This isn't about the money!" At least not for the McCoys. And not completely for her, either.

He stepped close, nearly overwhelming her with the size of his body and his torment. "You're the one who said I owed them."

Realizing the magnitude of her blunder, all she could do was sputter, "But—but—"

"There are no buts about it, Miss Sullivan. I'm my own man, and if this—" he held up the printouts "—is what it takes to prove it, then so be it." He straightened. "I'll leave it to you to deliver the news to the McCoys. My lawyer will deliver the check."

He gave a cursory tug on his hat. "Goodbye, Miss Sullivan. Oh, and watch that door. It tends to hit you in the rear on your way out."

Alison stared at him for a stunned moment, then turned and left the bank. She didn't know what was worse—the fact that Mitch felt driven to do something so drastic to avoid what she'd been sent for, or that she actually admired him for doing it.

"NEVER PARTICULARLY CARED for redheads, myself," Carl Mendoza mused from somewhere behind the thick black mustache that matched his wide-brimmed hat in attitude as well as color. He'd finally broached the subject Mitch had known would eventually come up.

The fact that Carl had offered to help him repair the close fence line rather than work on the busted ATV had tipped Mitch off that Carl had decided to ask him about what was going on. Mitch didn't toss women off his ranch every day. Refuse to continue dating them when all they wanted to do was spend his money, yes.

Since he was about to be without much money, that shouldn't ever be a problem again.

He jerked tight the wire they were fastening to a new post as the reminder of the decision he'd made the day before tightened what felt like barbed wire around his guts. But he refused to owe any debt outside of what he owed to the bank on this ranch.

The fact that he'd been seething with anger and frustration over what he had to do since he'd returned from town yesterday had probably tipped Carl off that something serious was up.

He saw Carl glance at him before he sunk a cleat over the wire and into the post with a hammer, his dark eyes worried.

Suddenly Mitch's navy-blue T-shirt became uncomfortable and started to bug him where it stuck to his sweaty back. He hated being under scrutiny, but he hated worrying Carl more.

Mitch released the now-secure wire and blew out a breath. "I like 'em just fine as long as they're not trying to tell me what I should do."

With a grunt of agreement, Carl returned the hammer to its spot on his tool belt with a spin like it was a six-shooter. He picked up his end of the piece of wood run through the spool of barbed wire and waited for Mitch to pick up the other end. They carried it to the next post hole already dug beside another old post that needed to be replaced and restrung, tromping through the brittle sagebrush rather than trying to dodge it.

They set the spool down just past the hole, and Carl picked up the new round fence post. "She didn't look like a BLMer."

Mitch snorted as he guided the end of the post toward the deep hole scant wider than the thick post. "No, Miss Sullivan doesn't work for the BLM." And Mitch certainly had never had a problem with the Bureau of Land Management serious enough to warrant bodily force.

"A lawyer?" Carl asked, still fishing.

As much as Mitch relied on and trusted the first man he'd hired to work on the ranch after he'd bought it, he couldn't bring himself to tell Carl what was really going on. That so much of Mitch's life had sprung from a huge cover-up.

But since Mitch's decision to pay back the money would affect Carl's security as much as his own—if the beef market bottomed out, the lack of any cash reserves would bankrupt them—he had to tell him some of it.

Mitch straightened and planted his hands on his hips. "A representative of a whole bunch of lawyers."

Carl hoisted his end of the post up onto his shoulder. His green cotton work shirt bunched beneath it, and he had to tilt his head to keep the post from knocking his black hat off. "Oh?" He said it casually enough, but Mitch could see the worry on Carl's weathered face. It made him look much older than forty.

Regret gave Mitch a bad taste in his mouth as he went

to put his shoulder under the post to help. "Yeah. Seems I owe someone. Going to take a chunk of change to make them go away."

Carl grunted and lifted the fence post over his head. "You've got a fair chunk of change on the hoof. Won't kill us to start over again. Sell 'em and be your own man again."

Exactly what every cowboy wanted to be. "I don't think it'll get that extreme, but I was pretty much thinking along those lines." His burdened lightened a bit with Carl's support, Mitch heaved the post into the hole and went down on one knee to guide it home.

"Mr. Smith!"

Mitch reared back, and with Carl having already let go, the heavy, unsecured post klunked into the side of Mitch's head with stinging force, knocking his cowboy hat cockeyed. He growled and stood upright, pushing the post straight in its hole again with one hand and straightening his hat with the other.

Carl murmured, "Redheads."

"Mr. Smith! Mitch!" Miss Sullivan called again as she picked her way over the tufts of grass and around the sagebrush toward the fence line.

She was back in her black jeans and the long-sleeved black blouse. The thick, shin-high sage blocked his view of her feet, but the care she took walking probably meant she was still wearing those ridiculous stiletto-heeled boots of hers. Clearly she'd packed light for her little jaunt to Colorado.

Mitch had thought for sure she'd headed for Missouri—make that *Mizzura*—to deliver his message to her employer after she left the bank yesterday. Just like he'd fled out here to the fence line first thing this morning after spending a miserable night figuring how best to mortgage everything he'd spent the last six years acquiring while still being able to make the monthly payments on the mortgage he already had. He'd cut off a hand before he gave up his great-grandfather's ranch.

When she reached them, she tucked her long, curly hair behind one delicate, perfectly shaped ear and smiled a smile that put the bright morning sunlight to shame.

"Damn." Carl softly expressed what Mitch was feeling low in his belly. Okay, fine. The woman was straight-up beautiful. Definitely too bad they hadn't met some other way.

She extended a hand to Carl. "Hi. I'm Alison Sullivan."

Carl wiped his hand on his faded blue jeans before taking hers. Her skin was startlingly fair against his leather-brown hide. "Carl Mendoza."

"Nice to meet you." She sounded and looked sincere as she shook his hand, but when she let go and turned to Mitch, there was a definite hard glint in her thickly lashed blue-green eyes. "I know you believe otherwise, but I still have a job to do."

Mitch lowered his chin. "What I believe is that you're on my property again."

Carl shifted back a step. "You know, I should probably get to fixing that busted four-wheeler."

Mitch nodded vaguely, glad for Carl's intuitiveness. "That's fine."

Mitch kept his attention on Miss Sullivan as she watched Carl climb on the one working ATV, tool belt and all, and head back in a dusty cloud toward the equipment building on the other side of the house.

Though he hadn't meant to study her, he noticed the dark circles under her eyes and the tightness at the corners of her full mouth.

He ignored the poke of sympathy. "I told you our business was done, Miss Sullivan."

She took a deep breath and looked at him again. "Not until you agree to come back to Missouri with me."

He opened his mouth to argue, but she held up a hand and stopped him.

"What you tell Joseph McCoy when you get there is up to you, but I need you to do it in person. I was hired to deliver that letter to you and escort you to the McCoy estate outside of Dependable." She crossed her arms tightly under her distracting breasts. "Our business won't be done until that happens."

His blood warmed by more than his anger, which fueled said anger more, Mitch jerked his attention back up to her eyes. "I'm not leaving the Circle S." Especially now that he had a second mortgage to secure.

"The McCoys deserve—"

"I don't give a rip about the McCoys, Miss Sullivan. I don't know them, and I don't care to. I won't stand for someone trying to turn my life upside down. My place is here, not with a bunch of people who wouldn't give a rip about me if it weren't for a dead guy's will. End of story, end of our business."

Her face paled, making the bruised-looking skin beneath her eyes more pronounced. Unable to ignore the poke guilt gave him this time, Mitch inhaled deeply to try to calm down.

She nearly whispered, "That dead guy was your father."

His heart twisting for all the lies the people he loved had had to tell, Mitch forced out his next words. "Ed Smith is my father. He earned the title."

"Joseph McCoy has the right to earn—"

"Goodbye, Miss Sullivan." He turned his back on her desperation and his own pain and went back to setting the fence post in its hole. "And just so you know, my property extends to that gravel road over there. Trespassing is against the law."

Out of the corner of his eye he saw her turn and head toward her rental truck. He listened until he heard her vehicle roar back to the main road and drive away. Good. Maybe that had done the trick. While he admired her work ethic, this was his life.

The only life he'd ever wanted.

He lost himself in the hard physical labor that gave him such satisfaction much the way he had before, working well past lunch. But working alone, he'd only progressed four fence posts down when a loud, artificial shriek rent the stillness and brought his head up from the wire he was pulling tight around the post.

The white rental truck was back.

"Mr. Smith!"

And Miss Sullivan was standing in the bed of the truck.
With a bullhorn.

Mitch couldn't help but smile at the woman's tenac-
ity and ingenuity. Since she was still on the gravel road,
she wasn't trespassing, but she wasn't leaving him
alone, either.

"Mr. Smith, I was remiss in not explaining to you the
reason for Joseph McCoy's desire for your immediate
presence that goes beyond the need to execute the terms
of his son's will. He's turning seventy-five years old
soon, and nothing would mean more to him than having you and…and, ah…those who share your, er, circumstances with him to share in the event. He's just an
old man who doesn't want to miss out on a moment
more of…of what he's already missed."

Mitch shook his head at her change in tactic and
hammered down the fastener over the wire. Sure, he
tried to be kind to old ladies and puppies, but he had a
hard time feeling sorry for a multibillionaire, seventy-
five years old or not. He unwrapped the now-secure
wire and went back for the next strand, nevertheless impressed as hell by a certain redhead.

The bullhorn crackled. "It's the least that he deserves,
having given so much to others his whole life."

She launched into a dissertation on the charities and
community works the McCoy family supported, from
donating a corporate jet to facilitate organ transplants

to providing college scholarships to entire classes of children.

She kept it up nonstop for the amount of time it took him to finish stringing one more fence post and the setting of another. While he normally would have taken a break, he could be just as stubborn as she was. He hoped she had sunscreen on that fair little nose of hers.

Unfortunately, though distorted, her husky voice grew even more so through overuse and started to wreak havoc on his concentration. He caught his leg in the barbed wire twice, once ripping his jeans on the inside of his thigh, and bashed his gloved thumb with the hammer.

And he noticed Juan and Richie ride in from checking on some of the calves they'd treated the other day. They were at least a couple hundred yards away, but he couldn't tell if they could hear Miss Sullivan or if they'd come over to see what was going on. Carl had been conspicuously out of sight the entire time.

So far his tormentor had studiously avoided mentioning any specifics about his relationship with the McCoys, but she had to be running out of material.

He set his jaw and went to his truck parked where he and Carl had unloaded the last of the new posts. He closed up the back and Miss Sullivan fell silent. He climbed into the cab, started the engine, then turned the truck around and drove slowly over the rough ground along the fence line to the road and the gate separating their two rigs. He left his truck running and got out, not bothering to open the gate but just climbing through it to reach her.

She watched him from the bed of the rental truck, the white bullhorn held in front of her as if she was afraid she might have to use it to call for help.

He stopped at the side of the truck bed and looked up at her. "You're not going to quit, are you?"

She shook her head, sending long, slender red curls into her face. "I thought I'd made that pretty clear." Her voice was downright sultry in its roughness.

He blew out an exasperated breath and planted his hands on his hips. "If I agree to talk to you about this, in a normal, civilized way, will you quit?"

"I'll quit bugging you with this." She raised the bullhorn.

He snorted. At least she was honest. "Good enough for now. Do you like beef?"

She raised coppery brows.

"Come back Friday night and I'll grill you a fresh Angus steak. We're sort of known for it out here." He turned and walked back to his truck without waiting for her answer.

It was probably stupid of him to invite the enemy back into his camp, but he could think of worse things than spending an evening with a woman who looked like Alison Sullivan.

Chapter Four

Alison eyed the open gate wryly as she drove past it early Friday evening. She'd halfway expected to find it still latched closed and locked against unwelcome intruders such as herself.

She'd realized too late that when Mitch had invited her to dinner she should have demanded his word as a cowboy, the oath of the Old West or something to guarantee that he would talk to her over dinner in exchange for her leaving him alone until then. He'd been so stubborn up to that point, she should have doubted his capitulation a little more.

But the gate stood open, so he was at least willing to let her onto his property again. Thank goodness for small favors.

She readjusted her grip on the steering wheel as she slowly approached the house, not surprised to find her fingers stiff and sore. She'd had a stranglehold on the wheel all the way from the quaint little motel on the other side of Whiskey Ridge where she'd rented a room.

Not even the beauty of the distant Rocky Mountains to the west, appearing closer than they were thanks to a haze-clearing breeze, could relax her. She was as nervous as all get out, and not entirely from the lack of faith in her luck. Vanity sucked.

The memory of the look in Mitch's eyes when he'd asked her to have dinner with him had made sleep difficult to come by and actually had her fussing over which of her two outfits to wear tonight. She'd gone as far as hand-washing them both, forcing her to hang around in her hotel room all day yesterday in her underwear, the curtains drawn and the Do Not Disturb sign out.

Fortunately, in this dry air, it hadn't taken long for her jeans and shirts to dry strung over the discolored tub.

No matter how many times she'd replaced *Wheel of Fortune* with *It's Not a Date* as she watched the game show, she was still preoccupied with her appearance.

Talk about a waste of time. Especially when the only thing she'd succeeded at so far this trip was annoying Mitch. Swaying him with looks alone would be a tad unlikely, but she did have her pride.

She blew at a wayward curl in disgust and pulled into the space between the deserted corral and the house. She already knew from experience about pride coming before a fall. Still had the bruises to prove it. But she'd gotten up, and planned to stay there. So she put the truck in Park and vowed not to give another thought to the black jeans and black short-sleeved T-shirt she'd worn instead of the long-sleeved knit top in a lame attempt to mix up her wardrobe a bit. Or the fact that she'd applied more than her usual modest amount of makeup or that she shouldn't have let her hair fly.

She needed to stay fixed on her goal. Since she seriously doubted Mitch would give her a second chance like this to change his mind, she'd decided to fall back on the argument that if he just got this trip to Dependable over with, he could return to his life all the sooner.

And she could return to hers, minus the threat of impending bankruptcy and the haunting fear that Scott's parting taunt might be true.

She could do this.

Confidence pumping through her, she turned the engine off, grabbed her black satchel purse and the bottle of red wine she'd brought, then climbed out of the car. She squinted against the low-slung sun that had yet to be overtaken by a gathering band of clouds approaching from the south and scanned the front of the house and surrounding area. No sign of her host. Or anyone else.

Didn't matter. She'd camp out on his porch if she had to. She slammed the truck door shut and marched toward the house. As she approached the steps, the screen door squeaked open and Mr. Mitch Smith elbowed his way out, drying his strong hands on a red-and-white-checked dish towel.

That matched his frilly apron.

Alison halted and blinked up at him. Only a man with as much manliness as this guy could come away looking the epitome of every food-loving woman's ultimate fantasy in an apron like that.

Minus the white button-down shirt and tan jeans, of course.

The thought made her mouth dry and her pulse race.

But allowing his McCoy masculine beauty to make her heart go pitter-patter was just plain stupid. She was here for one reason and one reason only. She couldn't forget that.

She smirked. "Nice apron."

He smirked right back, spreading his arms wide. "Thought you'd like it. My mom left it here for when she comes to visit and goes on a baking spree."

Which might not be as often now that he knew his mom had lied to him. The same empathy she'd felt that first day flared.

Doubting Mitch would appreciate her sympathy, she joked, "I thought maybe you'd picked up on Mabel's fashion sensibilities."

His chuckle and wide, toothy smile made her heart switch from pitter-patter to *whomp-whomp*. Great.

"I've learned the hard way that the splatters from my secret barbecue sauce don't wash out." He inspected the unprotected rolled-up sleeve of his white button-down shirt. "And my red shirt was dirty."

"Have to say I'm surprised I rate a clean shirt." She noted his damp hair, the thick waves finger-combed back from his face. "And a shower."

"The shower was as much for me as you. I finished

that fence line repair and stunk to high heaven. As far as the clean shirt goes…" He shrugged. "You certainly can make a decent argument to the contrary, but my mother at least taught me some manners."

His small smile and acknowledgement that he'd previously treated her in a less-than-mannerly way was the damnedest apology she'd ever received. And his acknowledgement that his mother could have given him more, namely the truth, kept her from commenting.

He flicked the towel toward the bottle of wine in her hand. "What do you have there?"

She self-consciously hoisted the bottle. "My mother taught me to never come to dinner empty-handed. And since I couldn't bring her standard tuna casserole…"

"Unnecessary, but thanks."

She mimicked his shrug. "Mabel said it was good. And on sale." Something that wouldn't matter to him once he accepted that he was a McCoy. If she did her job well, it wouldn't matter so much to her, either.

He opened the screen door for her. "Come on in." He held the door so she'd have to pass close to acres and acres of broad chest and self-assured man.

Alison's confidence promptly deserted her. She jerked her purse higher on her shoulder and climbed up the stairs to the porch, anyway. With just the barest smile of thanks tossed in his direction, she kept her attention on where she was going rather than on Mitch, but still managed to smack into the door frame opposite him as she went through.

"Careful," he cautioned, reaching out and grabbing

hold of her upper arm to steady her and guide her through the doorway.

The feel of his strong hand on her only managed to unsteady her further.

In an attempt to hide her reaction to his touch, she shrugged her black satchel off her shoulder. "Darn purse." She glanced back at him. "Always getting in the way."

"Hmm." He nodded as he followed her into the house, easing the screen door closed behind him. "Then you'd better put it on the table there. Can't have you hurting yourself." Amusement tinged his deep voice.

Alison bit back a groan as she went to the small half-moon table snug against the wall between the opening to the small living room and the base of the stairs. On the table's top sat a shallow Native American pottery bowl corralling a jumble of keys on various key chains—a bright yellow one that looked like it'd float and one that would clip on a belt the most noticeable. Next to the bowl lay a well-worn brown leather wallet and a handful of change.

She could imagine Mitch barreling down the stairs and scooping up his wallet and keys on his way out the door, or dumping them the second he came back in, exhausted from a long day. The sort of domestic scene she'd looked forward to but never really had. She brushed the maudlin observation aside and set her too-big purse down on the floor next to the table.

"Here, let me take that wine." He appeared right next to her, smelling not only of spicy after-shave but an even more heavenly scent of barbecue sauce, and gently took the wine bottle from her hand. "I'll open it and give it a second to breathe."

Wondering how a cowboy living out in the middle of nowhere knew what should be done with red wine, she offered apologetically, "I'm not sure it'll make much difference."

"Well, it can't hurt. Go ahead and make yourself comfortable in there." He nodded toward the small living room. "I have a couple more things to get ready before I put the steaks on."

Alison glanced into the living room, her gaze catching on the photo he'd been staring at that first day atop the mantel. She could tell now that it was a picture of a group of people, but that was about it. As much as she'd like to get a good look at it, she'd come here to change this guy's mind—something that couldn't be done with him in the kitchen and her out here. The urge to snoop heartened her, though. She might be suited to this P.I. gig, after all.

She smiled at him and said, "I'll come with you. I can give you a hand."

He hesitated a moment, then nodded. "Sure. Okay. Kitchen's back this way."

Having already made the circuit of the house on the outside, Alison pretty much knew the layout, but she followed along. Instead of leading her down the hallway that bisected the house, he took her through the doorway opposite the living room and into the dining room, pausing long enough to retrieve a corkscrew from a sideboard.

The highly polished antique table, chairs and the matching sideboard looked more like what she would have expected of the furnishings in a house such as this. Lyrical Victorian styling tempered by prairie sensibility. Pretty but still usable. She liked it instantly, even though the room lacked any sort of superficial decorating touches just as the other rooms she'd seen through the windows had.

She followed him through a second, narrower doorway that opened into the kitchen.

Alison paused and inhaled deeply. "What an incredible smell." It was sweet and savory and made her mouth water and her stomach growl.

After pulling the cork from the wine bottle and setting both on the whitewashed wooden breakfast table in the center of the kitchen, Mitch headed for the very modern, high-end stovetop. "My secret barbecue sauce." He picked up a wooden spoon and stirred the steaming contents of a small saucepan. "I normally only make it for ribs or chicken, but..." He trailed off and shrugged with an air of generosity like he was gifting her with the back forty.

Alison's jaw tightened. He was probably hoping to soften the fact that he had no intention of cooperating with a little culinary bribery. She resisted the urge to snort. She didn't love barbecue that much.

She didn't love anything that much. This was her

chance to prove herself capable and she wasn't about to budge.

She came farther into the roomy kitchen, noting the tidy counters and laundry nook to the right of the back door. Even the green-and-black-checked dog bed between the nook and the door looked well cared for. "You really didn't have to go to such trouble, Mr. Smith—"

"Mitch," he asserted with greater conviction than he had the first time in the hardware store. "And it's the least I could do."

Everything in Alison waited for him to add, *Since I fully intend to send you packing without what you came for*—namely his agreement to accompany her—but the admission never came. He just kept stirring the sauce.

He seemed unaware of her intense scrutiny, seemed unaware of *her,* until he pointed with his thumb at the refrigerator across the kitchen from him. "My mom's three-bean salad only needs to be taken out and dumped in a bowl. If you like, you can handle that for me. Oh, and go ahead and take the steaks out of there, too."

"Sure." Very aware of the intimacy of the situation, as if she was a friend over for dinner, not a professional on the job, she went to the refrigerator and opened it. The contents of the fridge distracted her. Along with the prerequisite beer, there were salad dressings and sauces, a roast waiting to be cooked, a full meat drawer, as well as apples and oranges in the fruit compartment and assorted veggies in the vegetable keeper.

"Wow." She glanced over her shoulder at him. "I expected the half case of beer, but I didn't expect you to be so well stocked with other stuff, considering you're a bachelor living alone."

He turned to look at her, a blond brow raised. "What makes you so sure I live alone?"

She scoffed and returned her attention to the refrigerator. "It's my job to know." She took the mason jar of mixed beans and the clear, plastic-covered plate holding two huge steaks out of the refrigerator and closed the door with her elbow.

He reached into a cupboard next to him and took out a clear glass bowl. "Mabel told you I'm not shacking up with anyone, didn't she?"

She choked on a laugh. "No. At least not in so many words. But she did get rather chatty after I was in her store with you." Alison set the steaks down on the counter next to Mitch, then tried to open the jar of beans.

After watching her struggle unsuccessfully to get the lid off the jar, he reached for it. She turned away and kept twisting until the seal surrendered with a satisfying pop.

Smiling in triumph, Alison continued, "She said it's about time you had something in your life that didn't have something to do with dirt or hooves."

He laughed, a deep sound that startled her with its fullness. And she was close enough to notice a slight dimple in one cheek. "Well, Mabel does know me, I guess."

Alison forced her attention back to the beans, dumping them into the bowl. "She also worries about you now that your men all have families to go home to."

The smile dimmed slightly and he returned his attention to the sauce. "That they do. Juan managed to save enough to be able to bring his mother and younger sisters up here from Mexico. Richie has his own place now just down the road, and Carl finally got the nerve to ask his girlfriend to marry him." He glanced at the digital clock on a small black radio next to the stove and let out a soft chuckle. "Teresa is probably getting back at Carl by dragging him out onto the dance floor at the festival right about now."

He turned the burner beneath the sauce off. "I keep the fridge stocked because the guys all still camp out here when needed, like when we were bringing those calves down from where they were pastured to tend to them."

She almost commented that he had a family to go home to now, also, in the McCoys but remembered what he'd said about his parents and half sisters. He felt he had more than enough family already. She didn't want to put him on the defensive more than she already had.

He lifted the lid on another small saucepan simmering on the back burner, releasing the most heavenly sweet smell, and stirred the contents.

Alison stepped closer to see into the pot. "Mmm. What's that?"

"My secret chocolate sauce. For my secret dessert."

"You're just chock-full of secrets," she teased, thinking of the barbecue sauce.

His expression turned stony. "No. I'm not."

Alison swallowed her chagrin. Of course he'd think of the secrets surrounding his paternity. And wouldn't see any humor in the situation. He was the victim of secrets, not the perpetrator. She silently berated herself. At this rate she'd never gain his cooperation.

The mood definitely affected, he replaced the lid on the chocolate sauce and turned the heat off. "If you'll grab those beans, we can go out back."

He picked up the pot containing the barbecue sauce by the handle and pulled a marinade brush from a stainless-steel utensil holder next to the stovetop, then grabbed the plate of steaks and headed for the open back door.

Alison followed.

"Look out, Hoss," he said.

The pile of black, white and light brown fur she'd avoided the other day lurched to life and suddenly became an Australian shepherd. A very old Australian shepherd. The dog's movements were slow and rickety. Except for its hind end, which wagged in a blur of doggy pleasure.

"Good boy," Mitch crooned before he slowly pushed the screen door open, allowing the dog time to move out of the way. "Say hello to Alison, Hoss."

Hearing him say her name as he would a friend's startled her, and the jolt of pleasure riding on the heels of her surprise worried her. All he'd done was say her name, for heaven's sake. This was business. Crucial—critical—business. She couldn't forget that.

She bent to greet the old dog as he wagged his way in front of her. She'd intended to do nothing more than pat the dog's head, but his warm, kind eyes drew a smile and a "Well, hello, Hoss," from her despite her determination to be all business. She stroked his silky head and scratched behind his ears, earning a lolling-tongue doggy smile.

"Hoss was my first employee at the Circle S." Mitch drew her attention as he went to the propane barbecue grill set against the house, the grill's cover folded on the porch next to it. "The last people to own this place before the bank took it over had up and left him here. I tracked them down to make sure it wasn't an accident. It wasn't."

He shook his head in obvious disgust. "They'd just left him to fend for himself. Fortunately, the second I found out the place was available, I jumped at the chance to buy it. So by the time I got out here and found him, he hadn't been on his own for too long."

"Why do you say you jumped at the chance to buy it?"

Mitch set the saucepan and plate down on the side of the grill and lifted its lid. "This ranch had belonged to my mother's grandfather. Her stories of visiting him here were what made me want to go into ranching in the first place. Seemed like fate when his ranch became available again."

He nodded at the dog nuzzling at her to keep her attention. "Hoss and I made a good team for a lot of years, but now he gets to enjoy retirement here on the back porch." The steaks sizzled and smoked when he slid them onto the preheated grill. Using the marinade brush, Mitch dabbed the steaks with the aromatic barbecue sauce until Alison's mouth watered from the mingled scents.

Hoss lost interest in Alison and followed his nose to his master. The old dog's hearing might be shot, but clearly his sense of smell worked just fine.

"Forget it, buddy." Mitch stuck the brush in the saucepan and lowered the lid on the grill. "Go lie back down." It was more of a kindly suggestion than a command. He pointed at the doormat Alison was still standing on, so she let the screen door close and stepped aside as the dog complied.

"He really is a good dog," she said, but she was more impressed by Mitch's kindness.

"He sure is." Mitch came toward her. "Why don't you go ahead and put those beans on the table and have a seat."

She turned toward where he was indicating and her jaw went slack. A little table for two, beautifully set with everything including several small, lit candles in clear glass votives, occupied the corner of the porch beside the hot tub. Her heart started to *whomp-whomp* again.

With raised brows, she glanced at Mitch. "I not only rate a clean shirt, but a white tablecloth?" Oh, man, this was beginning to look a whole lot more like a date than a business dinner.

He took the bowl of beans from her on his way by.

"I use this table for all sorts of things. Like cleaning fish. I scrubbed it best I could, but trust me when I say it needed covering."

She inched closer as if she were approaching some forbidden fruit. And boy, was she. The man could tempt the most scorned of women. But her goal here was not to have a romantic encounter with Mitch Smith. She was here to avoid bankruptcy. And the shame of proving the only two men to have ever mattered in her life right.

"Candles?"

He found a place for the beans in the middle of the table. "To keep the bugs away. They're citronella. My sister Megan swears by them. I figured I'd better use them before she comes over from Denver for another visit. She'd notice if I hadn't. Same with the tablecloth."

He flicked at its edge. "She and Michelle say they're trying to civilize me, but frankly I think they just want an excuse to buy stuff from Pottery Barn."

She laughed, all the while silently cursing him. Enjoys cooking, kind to dogs, a thoughtful brother... Enough already!

He pulled out one of the folding wooden chairs for her. His apparently unconscious chivalry made him far more civilized than most men who'd lived their entire lives in the supposedly civilized urban hubs of the world. Not that she'd encountered all that many.

Though the forever romantically wounded part of her shouted a warning that he was exactly the type of guy she could really, really like, she ignored it and accepted his gallantry by taking the offered seat.

She was made of stronger stuff than that.

As Mitch helped her move her chair close again, a gust of wind whipped at the edges of the tablecloth and made the flames of the squat, yellowish candles dance so much they blackened their glass votives.

He grumbled, "If this wind keeps picking up, we won't have to worry about bugs, just our food blowing away."

"It's not that bad. And it's been so warm, it feels good."

Mitch stepped to her side and planted his hands on his hips, surveying the clouds building on the southern horizon. "Weather's definitely changing, that's for sure." He shifted his gaze to the table and gave it the same thoughtful inspection. "Let me go get that wine. It can breathe all it wants on its way to our stomachs."

Alison laughed and nodded her approval, then inspected the table herself after he went inside. Whether she'd ever need it or not, Alison's mother had seen to it she had the ability to set a fancy table, so she knew how a table should look.

Admiration for Mitch continued to grow. His sisters would be proud. The place settings were perfectly laid out. The plates were plain white and the utensils simple in design, but they were of good quality. Probably from his sisters, too.

There were two wineglasses ready to go, so she hadn't overstepped her bounds by bringing wine. He had obviously planned to serve some. The knowledge rekindled her apprehension. Both of them had thought to use a little vino to smooth the path toward getting their way.

Whatever his intentions for the evening were, she wouldn't let him keep her from convincing him to come to Dependable.

Mitch came back out with the wine and filled her glass, then his own. Alison found herself staring at his large, tanned hands, bisected by little white scars that didn't mar them, but instead gave the impression of unflagging strength and capability.

She jumped when he spoke. "Let me give those steaks a flip so we can sit and chat for a while until they're done."

All righty, then. Chat, they would. About why he had to come back to Dependable with her by the first week in July.

She turned in her seat to watch him as he headed for the grill. "That would be great. Because while those steaks are already smelling delicious, I *am* here to talk, Mitch."

"And I agreed to do just that. So explain why getting me to Dependable is so all-fired important." He lifted the grill lid and succulent-smelling steam curled upward until snatched by the wind. The steaks sizzled when he flipped them.

"Because Joseph McCoy is legally bound to execute the stipulations in his late son's—your father's—last will and testament."

He slapped more barbecue sauce on the steaks with the brush. "My biological father," he grumbled.

"Correct." She acknowledged his emotional connection with the man who'd raised him. But hoping to play on those same emotions, she said, "That's not the only reason Joseph sent me to get you, however. As I told you before, his dearest wish is to have all of his newly discovered grandsons present at his seventy-fifth birthday party July 3."

"You've already told me all that. And it still doesn't answer why it's so important to *you*."

She blinked at his question, surprised by his probing. "That's not what I'm here to talk about."

He closed the lid and sauntered back to the table, settling himself in his chair like a man grateful for the chance to take a load off. "I know what you're here to talk about, Alison, but I also want to know a little more about you."

Wait a minute, she was supposed to be running this chat session. "Why?"

"I'm curious." His deep blue gaze roamed over her face and hair. Despite the flat light created by the accumulating cloud cover, his eyes glowed. "How could I not be?"

Stinging heat erupted on her upper chest and she was acutely aware of its migration toward her face. The man had the dangedest ability to disconcert her. She pulled in a fortifying breath. "I was hired to do a job, and I intend to do it."

He picked up his wineglass and swirled the deep red liquid. "But you almost act as if your life depends on it."

The close-to-the-mark statement had her reaching for her own glass, but she took a rather large drink instead of playing with it.

His continued intense scrutiny had her confessing, "In a way it does." She quickly amended, "At least as far as my business is concerned." He didn't have to know how messed up her personal life was, too.

"So there's actually a shortage of illegitimate heirs to millions to track down?"

She almost said, *not where the late Marcus McCoy is concerned,* but managed to keep the thought to herself. She didn't want to give him any more reasons to reject going with her than he already had.

When she remained silent, he mused, "You must have quite the track record to have been hired by a family as powerful as the McCoys."

She snorted before she could stop herself. How many times had she wondered about Joseph's reasons for contacting her? She'd eventually chalked his choice up to his well-known desire to support locally owned businesses in Dependable. He would have had to go out of town to find a more experienced P.I.

He raised his tawny brows. "No?"

She turned her head toward the barbecue grill and made a grand show of sniffing. "Those steaks smell done to me. You might want to check on them."

He eyed her for a minute, then unfolded himself from his chair and did as she'd suggested.

As he poked at the steaks and recoated them with barbecue sauce, she struggled with how much she should tell him about her situation, if anything.

While she loathed letting him know how desperate she was, it could help her. Any man who took in abandoned dogs and was considerate of his sisters might be willing to do something he'd prefer not to for someone in need. Or he might conclude she was a pitiful female not worth his time.

Not willing to risk the latter reaction, she went back to her game plan. "You know, you could probably get away with just going to Joseph's party. Then you could return here and get on with your life. It'd cost you a couple days. Three at the most. How bad could that be?"

"You don't let up, do you?" He closed the lid carefully and walked to the table. "Most people aren't this driven unless they're in serious debt."

She flinched, then tried to cover it by flicking her windblown hair away from her face.

He eased his big frame back into his chair and propped his elbows on the table, bringing him disturbingly close. The sweet, savory scent of the barbecue sauce clung to him and made her mouth water for more than one reason, which surprised her. The word *debt* usually made her feel as if she had a mouthful of sawdust.

"You know…" He mimicked her opener, his affected drawl like putting heat to butter.

Which she was apparently made out of.

"I might be more inclined to see things your way if I knew why you want it so bad."

She shifted in her seat. "You think that because I'm a woman, there must be some other reason besides commitment to the job I was hired for?"

He leaned closer. "Because you look scared, Alison. What's got you so spooked?"

Chapter Five

Mitch watched the color drain from Alison's face. Her reaction to what had been an offhand comment about her being in debt snared his interest. Had he hit the nail on the head? Or was she really just afraid of disappointing the all-powerful McCoys? Was their influence great enough that a failure to do their bidding could seriously cost her?

She fidgeted in her seat again. "I'm not scared. Or spooked."

Yeah, right. He gentled his tone the way he would with a skittish mare. "Forgive me for not being convinced, Alison. There's been a touch of desperation in those pretty eyes of yours from the get-go. Are you afraid of the McCoys?"

"No!" She leaned forward, her earnestness bringing their faces close over the small table. "Not at all."

The wind and the lemony scent of the candles lulled as if to say, *Take a whiff of this one, buddy.*

Even as he mentally snorted at the ridiculous thought,

he breathed in deep the slightly floral scent of her per-
fume and the richness of the red wine on her breath. His
hormones promptly bolted straight through the gate as
if he were a line stud turned loose on a herd of mares.
Thankfully he'd never been the type ruled by anything
south of the belt buckle.

She shook her head and sent auburn curls into her
face. She brushed them away with an impatient hand.
"The McCoys have been a godsend. Honestly. If Joseph
hadn't trusted me with this job, I wouldn't have been
able to put off Scott's creditors."

Every one of Mitch's biologically rooted competitive
instincts kicked into full alert, whether he wanted them
to or not. He blurted "Scott?" a little too sharply.

She blinked and he instantly reined himself in. She
was, after all, here with him, on his back porch, whet-
ting his appetite and making him forget that he'd asked
her here for the sole purpose of getting her off his back.

Color returned to her face in a rush, flushing her fair
skin like a day spent in the sun without a hat. She fid-
dled with her wineglass, turning it as if trying to decide
what side would be best to drink from.

Mitch took a sip of his own wine to make her think
he wasn't as interested in her answer as he really was.
He had no idea where all of this primitive stuff was coming from. Talk about inappropriate.

Finally, she shrugged and met his gaze. "Scott's the
weasel I foolishly married two years ago."

Mitch choked on the wine he'd been in the process

of swallowing. He coughed, then practically squawked, "You're married?" He never would have decided to use a little innocent romancing on the porch as a diversion if he'd known she was a Mrs.

She screwed up her face and her eyes sparked with indignation. "No! Not anymore. Hence the term *weasel.* He used our personal assets, including our new house and cars, to secure loans for his business. Right before he reduced our lives to the ultimate cliché and up and took off to Mexico with his receptionist."

As she shifted in her seat, lines appeared at the corners of her mouth. "I filed for divorce the day he finally called to let me know what he'd done." She dropped her gaze back to her wineglass. "Though it did take a long time for the divorce to be final without his cooperation."

Indignation of a much darker sort than she'd shown flared in Mitch. "You mean he took off with another woman but wouldn't give you a divorce?"

"Oh, no, he wanted the divorce, he just didn't want anyone—namely the people he owed money to—to know where he was. So I couldn't send him the papers I needed him to sign." She sighed and sat back. "Made for a fine mess."

A bone-deep urge to growl gripped Mitch. "Which included you being left holding the bag for his debt."

"Exactly." Her tempting red curls caught in the breeze again. "I know it's the best choice for some, but for me, twenty-eight is a little too young to declare bankruptcy."

He nodded, more in comprehension than agreement. Alison Sullivan wasn't the bad-to-the-bone, private investigator extraordinaire he'd thought she was, but rather simply a spurned woman in need of some fast cash.

The type of woman with an agenda.

Exactly the type he'd sworn never to let trot in his path again after he figured out what Krissi had really been after: his net worth.

She raised her chin and squared her shoulders. "Look, just forget I said anything."

"No, it's okay." He waved off her defensiveness. "And I do feel bad for the circumstances you've found yourself in." But it seemed women too often had some sad story. And he'd learned his lesson.

"I don't want or need your pity, Mitch."

"Just my cooperation."

The tension in her jaw plain, she gave a short nod. "Nothing but."

Something she wasn't going to get, but damn, he admired her spunk. And her glare was so adorable it made him laugh, despite their impasse.

Her glare deepened at his outburst.

He held up his hands. "Hey, how about we give the matter a rest and enjoy our dinner. Though I've probably reduced the steaks to beef jerky by now."

She watched him with wary eyes as he pushed his chair back. He paused and waited for her decision. He could see her struggle with what she wanted to do, the turmoil darkening her blue-green eyes and creasing her brow further.

Something shifted unexpectedly in his chest. He really did feel bad for her. Just how bad, he wasn't sure. And didn't care to find out.

It took a few heartbeats more, but finally her shoulders relaxed and the hard line she'd pressed her mouth into eased as the tension visibly left her. "Okay. For now."

"Good." He stood, grabbed his plate and headed for the barbecue, which fortunately wasn't smoking yet or smelling of burned steak. That softening inside of him toward her had him adding, "Because I really do want to get to know you."

"For heaven's sake, why?"

The incredulity in her tone made him glance back at her. She'd swiveled in her seat to watch him, one long, black jeans-encased leg stretched out. The slightly curved stiletto heel of her boot added to her shapeliness.

Okay, maybe he couldn't entirely blame any softening toward her on wanting to "get to know" her. She was mighty pretty. And he was a long way from dead.

He defaulted to part of the truth. "Because I admire your gumption."

She pulled in her chin. "My *gumption?*"

"Yeah." He rescued the steaks, putting them on the clean plate. "You sort of caught my attention with the bullhorn."

One side of her mouth curled upward. "That was the point."

Her hint of a smile heated him to a sizzle slicker than an open flame. Daring enough to want to experience a full-out sparkler, he added, "Besides, it's been a while since I've had the pleasure of a pretty lady's company."

She made a noise in the back of her throat and muttered, "Never would have guessed it after meeting that bank teller."

He made a noise of his own, definitely a rude one. "Krissi Torella."

She eyed him as he brought the plate of steaks back to the table. "That's right, Krissi."

"Been there, done that, learned my lesson." He let her choose which cut of meat she wanted, and wasn't surprised when she picked the smaller of the two.

"Oh?"

She sounded casual enough, but a little too much like he had when he'd been trying to hide his interest in her romantic entanglements. The thought that she was having the same elemental response to the prospect of competition puffed up his ego very nicely.

He settled back into his seat and put the plate with the remaining steak in front of him. "Let's just say you aren't the only one to hook up with somebody who had a vastly different vision of the future than you did."

She froze in the act of reaching for the three-bean salad, her eyes wide. "You and Krissi were *married?*"

Man, he sure hoped he hadn't looked that horrified when he'd asked her the same question. He scoffed and lifted the covering cloth from the sliced French bread. "No way. Not after I found out she was more interested in helping me spend my money than helping me build my dream."

Slender auburn brows inched upward as she served herself some bean salad. "Your dream being this ranch."

"Yep. Nothing but," he echoed her earlier statement. It was true now more than ever.

He accepted the bowl of beans when she passed it to him. Their fingers brushed and charged the air around them with potent electricity. A little too aware of his attraction to her, Mitch focused on scooping most of the remaining beans onto his plate.

She let out an audible breath. "I have to say I'm relieved."

"About what?"

"That you haven't been married."

His pulse quickened ridiculously over knowing his marital status mattered to her. He offered her the small bread basket, careful to avoid the candles flickering in the erratic breeze. "Why?"

She took the basket and helped herself to a slice. "I'd be appalled to have missed something that major in your background."

Ah, yes. The job. Mitch sawed at his steak, doing his damnedest not to be offended. "You did a background check on me, too? I figured you just had to find me."

She had the grace to duck her chin. "I thought it best to be thorough."

"Then it's a good thing I've never cheated on my

taxes." With his fork he stabbed at the piece he'd cut and stuffed it into his mouth.

She followed suit, but with far more grace and a re-markable amount of unconscious sensuality. Her eyes slid closed. "Mmm. This tastes incredible, Mitch. I've never had a steak this good before."

Her praise was bittersweet. If he couldn't find a len-der willing to give him a second mortgage on his spread, he'd have to sell his herd. "My *dream* was to restore my great-grandfather's ranch, my *goal* is to raise the highest-quality Angus around." More to him-self, he added, "If the banks don't cooperate, hopefully I'll be able to keep at least a few of the prime calves I have separated out to use as breeder stock to rebuild my herd."

She quickly swallowed and reached for his hand across the small table. "You don't have to get another loan or sell a single head, Mitch. Becoming a McCoy isn't supposed to cost you."

He pretended that he couldn't feel the warmth spreading from her touch. "I have no intention of be-coming anything other than what I am. I was raised to believe the name doesn't make the man." He gave a self-deprecating laugh. "With a last name like Smith it's al-ways been sort of a family joke."

He folded his fingers around hers, very aware of how rough his skin must feel against the satiny texture of hers and how aroused the simple contact with her made him. "It's the choices I make and how I live my life that defines who I am, and I refuse to allow anyone to believe otherwise."

Her big eyes clouded up much the way the sky was doing and tore at his gut like the storm building in the distance could tear up the landscape under the right conditions.

"We aren't supposed to be talking about that stuff, are we?" He gave her hand a brief squeeze. "While we finish our dinner, why don't you tell me how a beautiful girl like you decides to become a private investigator."

She slipped her hand from his with obvious self-consciousness and picked up her fork again. "I didn't have much choice. Sullivan Investigations was Scott's business. I was doing my best to be the good little home maker he wanted, even though I'd initially thought I'd be helping him in the office. But he said it would make him happier if I concentrated on making a home for us. When he took off…"

She started cutting at her steak as if the thing needed killing again. "I guess you could say I was too stubborn to simply close up shop and hand over what was left to the creditors."

"You? Stubborn? No," he joked to distract her from her painful memories, and was rewarded with a quick glance that had at least a little of the spark back in it. The fact that the spark was being generated by amusement filled him with the damnedest satisfaction.

She let up on the steak and even smiled slightly. "Amazing, I know, but true. I gave myself a crash course in the profession and went stumping for work around Dependable, mostly by trying to get into the Rolodex of as many lawyers as I could. And construction companies. They often have need for P.I.s to check out workers' compensation claims."

"Forgive me if I have difficulty picturing a woman with legs like yours *stumping* for anything."

She blushed and smiled a bit more, and Mitch's satisfaction edged toward something a heck of a lot more carnal.

"Well, what mattered most was my aim with a telephoto camera. Thankfully, I have a steady hand."

Imagining the sordid stuff a P.I. would normally be used for, he ventured, "And a strong stomach?"

"You've clearly never been to Dependable. It's known as the moral seat of the county, thanks primarily to Joseph McCoy. He's a very influential man." She punctuated the statement with a bite of steak.

Influential enough to destroy the budding career of a pretty P.I. if she failed him? Mitch pushed the disturbing thought aside. "And thanks to the not-so-moral Marcus McCoy, you've landed yourself the mother of all cases."

She held up her hand and chewed quickly, clearly intending to protest, but he cut her off.

"Sorry, my bad. That subject's off limits—"

She gulped down the meat. "But—"

"How about we finish our meal while just living in the moment and enjoying the scenery? From the looks of things, there's a storm brewing."

Those intelligent, stirring eyes of hers studied him for a moment, then she gave a quick nod and turned her attention to the thick band of pinkening clouds forming a dramatic backdrop for the horse corral he'd emptied earlier to keep the smell down. Why he'd thought to do so was beyond him, but now he was glad with the weather turning. The horses were happier out to pasture, and had a large lean-to shelter they could get under if needed.

Alison sighed. "It *is* beautiful."

He settled his own gaze on her profile. "I'll say."

She glanced at him, and he finally earned an honest-to-goodness grin from her.

It nearly knocked him out of his chair.

She rolled her eyes and muttered something that sounded like "cowboy charm," but her pleasure was still obvious and fed his own the way the wind feeds a storm.

They settled into a comfortable silence as they finished eating dinner, or at least as comfortable as his ever-growing attraction to her would allow. An attraction that wasn't merely physically based. Because not only did he admire and respect her determination, he actually liked her. A lot. Talk about a surprise.

Yeah, she had a sad story, but she was seeing it to her own end.

Luckily for him she'd be gone for good soon.

Though she'd only made it through half of her steak, bread and three-bean salad in the time it took him to slop up his plate, Alison sat back with a groan. "That was wonderful, Mitch. Thank you."

He caught and held her gaze. "You're most welcome. But we're not done yet." Her eyes flared and he did some grinning himself. "You better have left room for dessert. Don't forget I made up an extra-special batch of my secret chocolate sauce to drizzle over the world's best vanilla-and-caramel ice cream."

She groaned louder and covered her face. "Oh, no, I can't."

He stood and started stacking the plates and bowls. "Then you'll have to share mine, because you're not getting out of here without at least a taste. Which, I will say in completely egotistical fashion, is never enough."

She threw her head back and laughed, sweeping him up in her like a leaf in a flash flood. He shook off the melodramatic thought and started to carry what he could of the plates and bowls toward the house. Hoss anticipated the command and slowly got up and moved out of the way.

When he heard her gathering the utensils to help, he stopped and turned. "Oh, no you don't. You go around the corner and have a seat on the porch swing. It's stage center for watching the sunset."

She wrinkled her nose. "Porch swing? I don't remember any porch swing."

"That's because I don't leave it hanging up. The wind can get a hold of it and send it banging against the house right where my office is. Drives me nuts. But I thought you should see the Colorado sunset the second-best way, so I hung it up this afternoon."

"Dare I ask the first best way to see the Colorado sunset?"

He grinned and turned toward the house again, catching the bottom of the kitchen screen door with the toe of his boot to pull it open. "From the back of a horse, of course."

Her "duh" and throaty laughter followed him inside.

Feeling every inch the grinning fool over nothing more than having made a pretty girl in dire need of a smile actually laugh, he set their dinner things in the sink. After putting the bowl with the chocolate sauce that was more fudge than anything into the microwave to reheat it, he went to the freezer side of the fridge for the ice cream.

Taking her at her word, he filled only one bowl, though he pretty much maxed it out by the time he poured on a hearty helping of the chocolate sauce.

When he came back out, he saw that she'd taken what was left of the wine and their glasses with her. Inordinately pleased that she was getting into the spirit of the evening and was living in the moment, he sauntered past the barbecue and rounded the corner of the house.

The sight of Alison Sullivan sitting on the porch swing he'd built himself with his old dog curled beneath her stopped Mitch in his tracks.

Wow.

The wind was a little stronger on this side of the house and had her incredible dark red hair dancing around her head in a sexy cloud that made him damn near desperate to know how it would look spread out on one of his pillows.

He must have made a sound, because she turned her face from the equally fiery sky and smiled at him, something he found himself liking more each time it happened.

Since her hands were full with their wineglasses, she looped an arm around one of the swing's suspension chains and looked upward. "It's very slick how you just have to clip the chains to their anchors in the porch ceiling."

He moved to join her on the swing, purposely built for two. He'd never intended to fulfill his dream on his own. "Slick's my middle name."

"Lucky for me it's not, or I'd be spending a very enjoyable evening with the wrong guy." Her eyes seemed to glow in a way that had nothing to do with any reflection from the clouds, and she didn't seem to mind the close quarters.

He certainly didn't. Maybe he felt so comfortable in her space because he'd already invaded it that first day when he hauled her away from the house and dumped her in her truck. The first touch had been made. He mentally winced as he poked the spoon around in the ice cream. He owed her a decent apology for losing his cool with her like that. No amount of shock or upset warranted mistreatment of a lady. The fact that he liked her so much now made his earlier actions that much worse.

She eyed the full bowl. "So that's the secret chocolate sauce?"

The pleasure on her face had him stowing the formal apology for later. "Yep. The one you don't have room for." He made a show of loading the spoon up with a tempting mixture of ice cream and warm fudge.

Her tongue darted out to wet her lips. "It's surprising how quickly a body digests really good steak…."

He grinned at her. "Or how far a stomach can stretch?"

She nodded eagerly, humor dancing in her eyes. "That, too. I might have room for a bite. Or two."

He grimaced in mock regret, holding the loaded spoon level with his mouth. "Only brought one spoon. I was raised to take a lady at her word."

The noise she made let him know how much she believed that. "With two sisters? You have got to know that when it comes to dessert, 'no thank you' means 'two spoons, please.'"

Enjoying her wit, he laughed and played dumb. "Really? Well, that explains a lot." He shifted on the seat and offered her the spoon still filled with ice cream smothered in thick, dark chocolate sauce. "Then I guess this bite is yours, if you want it."

She gestured with the wineglasses she held in each hand and glanced at the bottle trapped between her legs. "Um…" She looked beneath her, at the spot Hoss had claimed.

He took pity on her. "Allow me." He offered her the spoonful, keeping the bowl beneath it. "Polish this off, then I'll go get myself that other spoon."

"That's all right," she said at the same time as she leaned toward him in preparation of accepting the bite. "You don't have to get another spoon. I don't mind sharing. As long as you don't have cooties."

"Cooties? I haven't had those since fifth grade."

"Good," she said on a laugh, then opened her mouth.

The second her tempting lips parted to accept the spoonful he knew he was doomed.

Because regardless of the fact that she was the type of woman he'd sworn never to let cross his path again, a whole bunch of parts of him were unquestionably attracted to *exactly* her type, all legs and wavy hair and grit tempered with humor.

And the next thing he knew, he was setting down the bowl of ice cream with the spoon and tasting his secret chocolate sauce on her lips.

Chapter Six

Alison had seen the hot look in Mitch's eyes despite the failing light, had felt the electricity arcing between them, building to a tumultuous intensity just as the clouds seemed to be doing in the distance. But she hadn't quite believed he was actually going to kiss her until his sensuous mouth captured her own.

And it was good.

His lips were gentle yet firm, restrained yet passionate, with the moist heat and shared taste of the sweetest chocolate trapped between them.

She hadn't made the conscious decision to use her feminine wiles to get Mitch to go with her to Dependable, but with his lips so coaxing against hers, she pushed her scruples aside and kissed him back. Anything was worth avoiding the failure Scott had predicted for her during that awful last phone call. And she wasn't going to give up the independence her doting father not only believed unnecessary but ultimately beyond the capability of such a sweet little girl. But she wasn't that trusting wife or little girl anymore, and the time to prove it had come.

The second she opened her mouth to Mitch, a jolt of hot, tingling pleasure coursed through her, tightening her muscles, her skin, everything from the inside out and sending her pulse racing.

Any and all calculation went flying away on the wind.

In its place emerged the need to take a risk, to really live for just a moment, despite being vulnerable on so many levels.

A rumbling moan came from low in Mitch's throat and he tilted his head, slanting his mouth more fully against hers. His tongue darted in to touch hers and ignited a hot throb deep in her pelvis. His fingers slid into her hair, massaging her scalp and holding her as he kissed her deeply, thoroughly. His tongue returned to stroke hers, his lips grinding against hers until she wanted the same sort of contact with all of him.

She reached for him, only to realize she still held two half-full wineglasses. And the bottle remained trapped between her legs. She squeezed it tight in the hope she wouldn't dump it and had to settle for looping her arms around Mitch's neck instead of touching his thick hair, his strong jaw or powerful shoulders.

Mitch's hand slipped from her hair and ducked beneath her arms, skimming the sides of her breasts as they made their way to her back. His touch seared through her black T-shirt and set her skin on fire.

She instantly ached from that barest contact and

arched into his hard, broad chest almost in the same instant that he pulled her as close to him as was possible on the porch swing. His pounding heart thrummed against her. Knowing he was as affected by the kiss as she was thrilled and moved her further.

As if the hunger in his kiss wasn't proof enough.

He withdrew to tilt his head to the other side, allowing her a second to pull in the breath of air that had just left his lungs. The thought made her weak. Then he sucked lightly at her lower lip and set her ablaze with desire.

His hands moved again. One slid upward, grazing the nape of her neck and pushing into her hair to cradle the back of her head, while the other held her just to the side of her breast. The near touch was more arousing. Or so she thought. She automatically shifted to chafe the hardened peak against his chest, sending tendrils of heat radiating through her.

Alison quivered and groaned her approval.

"Yeah," Mitch murmured in agreement against her lips, and leaned toward her, urging her backward into her corner of the porch swing. His hand protected the back of her head while his arm cushioned her as they eased down.

She had to remember to keep the wineglasses upright, a neat trick considering he'd effectively tipped her world on end. In a very, very mind-blowing way.

Then the wine bottle poked him.

"What…?" He broke off the kiss and slid his hand from her side to see what had come between them. He chuckled. "Oh." And took the bottle from between her legs.

"I was afraid Hoss might knock it over when he followed me here." She'd never heard that breathy voice from herself before. But she'd never responded to a man's kiss like this before, either. Not even with Scott. The realization stunned and—deep down—delighted her.

Good heavens, she was in trouble.

"We'll have to risk it." He set the bottle on the porch.

Alison unwrapped her arms from around his neck. "Probably should set these down, too."

Mitch blinked at the half-full wineglasses she held, then laughed. "I completely forgot you had those."

"Lucky for you, I didn't. Or you would have been taking a pinot bath."

"Hmm. Sounds intriguing." He waggled his brows as he took one glass and set it on the porch, followed by the other. "As long as you joined me, I'd be up for any sort of bath."

Images of wet skin on skin assaulted Alison and added to the impact of his hand returning to the side of her breast. Only this time he used his thumb to graze the swell through her shirt and bra. He made her want more. So much more.

"Mmm, Mitch. You make me feel so good."

Wearing an expression of heavy-lidded sexuality, he lowered himself close to her. "Better than my barbecue sauce?"

She inhaled deeply of the heavenly, tangy-sweet scent clinging to him. "As good as it was, yes, better than your barbecue sauce."

He brushed his lips over hers. "Better than my secret chocolate sauce?"

"Well…"

He laughed and crushed her mouth beneath a hungry kiss, effectively banishing all competitors, no matter how delicious. In a matter of minutes, Mitchell Davis Smith took her to a place where nothing else mattered with nothing more than a kiss. All that existed was this gorgeous, funny, surprising man and the way he made her feel.

Incredible.

SUCCUMBING TO THE URGE to know what Alison's throat tasted like, Mitch broke off the world-rocking kiss and worked his way below her jaw to the satiny skin of her neck. The power of the chemistry between them should have given him pause. While he hadn't expected her to recoil in revulsion from his first tentative kiss, the strength of her passion had taken him a little off guard.

Not to mention her ensuing enthusiasm.

Or his.

Free of the wineglasses, Alison delved deep into his hair, her slender fingers splayed. His enthusiasm blasted through the roof when she somehow managed to kiss his ear.

The woman sure could do a number on him. That thought did give him pause.

She had the power to mess up his world in more ways than one.

But when she sucked his earlobe and he shuddered

with pleasure, he told himself what was happening between them meant nothing because she was undoubtedly just using sex to try to change his mind about going to Missouri. Something that wasn't going to happen.

Because he wouldn't be affected in the long run, he allowed himself to continue to be swept away by the passion raging between them. She would, after all, be gone soon.

Moving upward, he gave her dainty little ear the same treatment she'd given his, then realized he'd slid his hand down to the hem of her T-shirt.

He froze. In his teens he'd made it a hard-and-fast rule never to dip for skin during the first make-out session with a woman. Not after his sister Megan had come home in tears from being seriously groped by a guy she'd only wanted to kiss. The idiot's clueless expression right before saying hello to Mitch's fist had helped Mitch decide what kind of man he'd wanted to be. As opposite from jerks like that as possible.

Besides, women tended to want to go further when it took time getting there.

He moved his hand away.

Alison's hands fisted in his hair.

He raised his head to see her face, to gauge if she was signaling him to stop everything—because he sure as hell would, without question—but she followed him upward and captured his mouth with hers. Man, she could kiss. The way she slid her soft, moist lips over his, teasing him with the tip of her tongue, really turned him on.

In a booming heartbeat he found himself rationalizing that there wouldn't be time to get very far with her because this was it. This was all the time they'd ever have with each other. And damn if *he* didn't want just a little more.

The man who'd walked away from this woman had to be a complete ass.

Mitch nudged his hand beneath the slightly stretchy black fabric of her T-shirt, but the second he made contact with her warm, satiny skin, he realized that he was the ass for thinking he could touch her and remain unaffected. So much passion and energy buzzed beneath her skin, searching for an outlet. While he knew in his gut he was just the man to be a conduit for her, he wasn't sure either one of them deserved the burns that would undoubtedly be left behind.

This was a mistake.

He slowly broke off the kiss. The pounding of her heart, easily felt by his hand on her rib cage, was only slightly outpaced by his and solidified his suspicion that there might be a price to pay for this particular sales pitch.

Might? Hell, he was already paying. And so would she.

Especially when he had to tell her, once again, that there was no way he was leaving his ranch at the beckoning of the family who'd bought his mother off so long ago. The ranch was who he was now, the one thing he could trust.

Not even an unprecedented physical connection with a woman like this was going to change that. He had no choice but to completely sever the connection now.

Better for her to think him a complete ass—make that a weasel—too.

ALISON'S NEED FOR OXYGEN finally won out over her body's need for contact with Mitch. With her eyes closed to further savor the previous moments, she allowed him to ease his mouth away from hers and lift his head from her grasp.

But she did make an inarticulate protest in her throat when he slid his warm, gloriously rough hand off her rib cage and out from beneath her T-shirt. She trailed her hands over his broad shoulders and down his rock-hard arms as he pulled them from her, encouraging him to stay put.

Stunned by the way Mitch made her feel—like a woman worth wanting—Alison had a hard time working up any remorse for making out with the newest and undoubtedly most reluctant member of the mighty McCoy clan. She felt too flipping good to give a ringed-rump about any line she might have crossed over, and she'd worry about her mission here tonight later. When it came to worry, there was always later.

They were both adults, and if she needed to, she'd jump up and down and holler her consent.

The image made her smile.

"That good, huh?" His deep voice resonated in her, though it held an odd flatness.

She slowly opened her eyes, but only far enough to

give him her best bedroom look. Assuming she actually had one. "Yeah, that good."

He turned to look at the now-dark horizon and moved farther away from her on the porch swing. The distancing was blatantly more than physical. She felt it as surely as she'd felt the heat they'd generated.

A shiver chased across her skin and a very deep hurt stirred. Alison grabbed the top of the swing's backrest and pulled herself upright. "No?"

He shrugged, still not looking at her. "Certainly better than Krissi when she tried to kiss me into doing what she wanted." His throat sounded in need of clearing.

Alison's jaw went slack. He was dismissing what had happened between them as an attempted manipulation on her part.

And it had been. At first. She snapped her mouth shut, thankful not enough light from the kitchen reached them to expose her hot face. How could she have been so stupid? How could she have thought for one second that he wouldn't see through her? Then something occurred to her.

"Hey, wait a minute. You kissed *me!*"

"But you kissed me back."

"Well, duh. Of course I kissed you back. Have you looked in a mirror lately? Listened to yourself? *Tasted your chocolate sauce?*"

He snorted, but she also detected a slight laugh. "I can use the same argument on you. How is a guy supposed to not kiss a woman who looks like you, with chocolate sauce dangling on those sexy lips like some sort of lure?"

Incredulous, she raised her brows high. "You think I was fishing for you?" She would have laughed if her conscience would have allowed it. But in her own defense she hadn't decided to try to manipulate him until after he'd kissed her. And she hadn't been able to stick with the plan for long. Any kissing she'd done had been honestly motivated.

He grumbled something that sounded like "If that dog hunts," then shrugged again.

She gasped at the accusation, but the sting of guilt for having contemplated the use of any and all weapons to get his cooperation significantly blunted her outrage. Not that he needed to know that.

Raising her chin, she retorted, "I think it's plain you were doing a little hunting of your own, *Mr. Smith.*" She started to count on her fingers. "The candles—"

"I told you those were citronella candles to keep the bugs away."

She ignored him and ticked off a second finger. "The table on the porch—"

"You're from out of town. Thought you'd enjoy the view."

That earned him a doleful look. "The wineglasses—"

"You're the one who brought the wine," he countered.

"But you didn't know I was bringing it. Besides, it's what people bring when invited to dinner at someone else's house."

"Around here you bring a slab of your best beef ribs or an extra tap for the keg."

She gave him a look to let him know that he'd made her point, exactly. Then she continued adding to her list of seduction props. "The secret barbecue and chocolate sauces—"

He huffed. "Can't blame a man for wanting to show off for a pretty lady."

The compliment sent a warm, soothing tingle through her that dulled the sharp edges of her ego a bit, but not enough to stop her. "And last but not least, this porch swing. Put up special for the occasion. If that's not proof of a hound dog—"

"But I'm a guy. That's what we think about."

She rolled her eyes. "Genetics at work. I'll have you know that the only thing I was thinking about was how wonderful this evening had been and what a great guy you turned out to be. But now I see you're just like every other guy. Thinking below the belt."

"And you're just like every other woman. Playing along with your hidden agenda—"

"Whoa. I don't have a hidden agenda. You've known from the get-go what I want." What she needed. To get this job done. "And for the record, I am *nothing* like Krissi."

"How do you know that with such certainty?" he blustered. "You barely met her."

"I had her pegged within the first five seconds. Trust me, I've met the type before." Namely her husband's receptionist, sitting at a desk outside his office every day, receptive to more than just clients.

The pain that had only poked at her pride earlier flared white-hot in the pit of her stomach. Mitch's kiss had opened a door she'd wanted to keep closed forever.

As she had in the past, she used her anger to muscle it shut. "I was surprised then that you'd gone for the sex-kitten type. But not as much now."

He ran a hand through his hair, worsening the mess she'd made of it with her fingers. "When I first met Krissi, she wasn't like that."

The regret in his tone fueled an irrational jealousy that had her lashing out with "Oh, so you drove her to it?"

A muscle flexed in his jaw. "No. She finally showed her true colors."

The hint of pain in his voice made her realize how cutting she'd been. How petty. She tried for a gentler tone when she asked, "Which were?"

He snorted in obvious disgust. "Green and platinum. All she was interested in was finding ways to spend my money on anything but the ranch. She wasn't the least interested in what I was working toward here."

"But she surely was interested in you." How could any woman not be? Unfortunately, Alison couldn't allow herself to be just any woman. She had to remain strong to stay her course and achieve the independence and success her father and Scott believed her incapable of.

"As long as I paid attention to her. Which grew to be

a real trick since she wasn't interested in spending much time here at the Circle S."

Wondering what sort of woman would attract a man like Mitch in the first place, she asked, "What was she like when you first met? And how far back are we talking?" How long had this other woman been a notable, if not important, part of his life?

Statistically speaking, Alison knew everything about Mitch from her investigation. Quite likely more than his close friends. She knew where he'd spent his youth, that he'd excelled at Colorado State, that he'd had only three speeding tickets—all promptly paid—and that he'd bought the Circle S ranch six years ago.

She *knew* him, yet she didn't. It was a very odd sensation.

"I met Krissi three years ago, when she started working at the bank in Whiskey Ridge. She seemed sweet. Kind of the girl-next-door type. The girl next door with a boozing, good-for-nothing dad who scared her sometimes."

Ah. "A damsel in distress in need of a white hat."

He slanted her a look, as if trying to decide if she was mocking him.

She wasn't. Though his Stetson or whatever kind of cowboy hat he wore was tan, given the right circumstances, she could easily see him riding to the rescue. He seemed that sort of guy.

Scott had been the love-'em-till-he-got-bored kind of guy, and she'd tried so hard to be what she'd thought he wanted. Agreeing to stay home despite wanting to help him with his business, trying to keep the perfect house that he'd claimed to want but never had time to come home to. Clearly it hadn't worked.

Mitch exhaled noisily and brought her out of her painful musings.

"After about six months, she started to change. I put up with her until the day I finally went to have it out with her dad."

"And you found out he wasn't what she'd said he was?"

"No, she hadn't lied about him. He was a drunk with a definite mean streak. But she had failed to mention that I was about to become one in a long line of sugar daddies she'd cleaned out before moving on."

"How could you be certain her dad wasn't lying to hurt her?"

"Oh, he wanted to hurt her, but he wasn't lying. He had proof. Pictures, letters. She'd brag about it to him, probably in some weird attempt to win his approval."

"What made you believe she planned to do the same to you?" Alison had to know if he was quick to condemn the damsels once he rescued them. That would place him in a different light entirely, one she would have no problem shunning.

He lifted one shoulder. "Didn't really matter if she planned to or not. Her dad's little revelation was the wake-up call I needed to acknowledge what I already knew. Krissi and I wanted two very different things out of life."

Alison told herself she shouldn't care, that it didn't

matter, that the answers were obvious, but the lingering feel of his mouth on hers had her asking to be sure, "Which are?"

"I want to live a quiet life out here, raising a family and making this ranch a success. She wants to live the town life where the only thing you invest in is your entertainment."

Alison shifted on the swing, making it rock slightly despite the fact that it was anchored by Mitch's feet planted firmly on the porch. Krissi had wanted precisely the sort of life Scott had used as bait to hook Alison.

She felt the ridiculous need to defend her own choice. "That's not that unusual a dream, you know. Especially for someone who grew up in the middle of nowhere. You grew up in Boulder—in town—so this great expanse—" she swept an arm toward the unbroken darkness in front of them "—is a fantasy come to life for you. For someone who grew up out here, it might seem like a prison."

He scoffed. "How could anyone feel imprisoned when they have nothing but freedom? No traffic jams, no neighbor standing in his upstairs window wearing a towel and looking down into your kitchen while you're trying to eat your dinner, no one to answer to besides the land and animals you depend on as much as they depend on you...."

She imitated his scoff. "How could you not feel imprisoned when the sheer distances involved out here are the walls? No store a couple of blocks away to run to for medicine when you get hit with the flu late at night, no neighbor for miles to help when it's something worse than the flu or you have an accident and you're bleeding, no vacation time because the land and the animals *never* stop depending on you…"

He studied her. "I think it's safe to say that you're a town girl through and through."

"That I am." At least now she was. And she had to successfully complete this job to keep it that way.

He shook his head, obviously pitying her again. "But it's such a reactionary way of life. There are so many factors deciding for you what you have to do. Out here, I decide what I do and when I do it. The choices are mine. That's something I refuse to give up for anyone, or anything."

Feeling bad for his situation with the McCoys more than she thought possible, she kept her tone gentle. "No one is asking you to give up more than a couple of days of your life, Mitch. Don't you think you've kind of blown this whole thing out of proportion?"

He ran a hand over his face, appearing suddenly bone tired. "No. I know in my gut it won't stop there. I read the letter, Alison. I'm supposed to take my 'place' in the McCoy family and business. I don't want it. The only way to make that clear to them is to pay back the million dollars."

With a sigh that spoke volumes about what his decision cost him emotionally, he leaned forward to rest his elbows on his knees. "The only way I can do that is to work day and night to find a lender who will give me a second mortgage, and sell anything else I can spare as quickly as possible."

"That won't leave you with much security."

"The only security I need is my land."

She couldn't keep herself from touching him, from smoothing her hand over the thick, dark blond hair curling under slightly just above his collar. Its softness was in sharp contrast to the hard set of his jaw.

"Speaking of working day and night..." He sat back, away from her touch. "I know I'm a louse for ending things like this, especially since I invited you here, and all. But you've reminded me of what I stand to lose. So I'd best get to it." He pushed himself to his feet and took a step away, setting the swing—and Alison's stomach— in motion.

She studied him as he planted his hands on his hips and stared out into the darkness. The smell of the approaching storm was plain on the wind that ruffled the hair she'd smoothed and seemed to claim him with a force she'd never be able to muster.

And she shouldn't want to even if she could. He was of the world she'd left for good. The prison she'd physically escaped. To go back would be to fail, to affirm archaic beliefs about daddies' little girls.

To succinctly prove Scott right.

She wouldn't do it. There was so much more to her than he'd ever acknowledged, let alone appreciated. Sure, he'd put on the romantic blitz until she'd thought he was the most wonderful man on earth and couldn't wait to marry him, but the fairy tale—the sense of victory in her escape—hadn't lasted.

And unfortunately, in nearly a year of courtship and eight months of marriage he had never made her feel as alive, as desirable, as Mitch had with a single kiss.

No man had.

Her gaze traveled over his cotton and denim-covered broad shoulders, strong back, perfect rear and long, muscular legs. In all fairness, none of the whopping four guys she'd had any sort of involvement with had looked like Mr. Mitch Smith, even while wearing his mother's apron. But it wasn't simply his physical attributes that set him apart. He'd been different with her eyes closed, too.

He breached barriers. Slipped past defenses. Made her want to hope.

Mitch heaved a sigh carried to her on the wind and turned back to face her. The darkness kept her from seeing more than the set of his square jaw and the big hand he extended to her.

Alison slipped her hand into his, the instant zing up her arm and down to her belly confirming his uniqueness. His grip was warm and intimate as he helped her to her feet, but he quickly broke the contact and bent to pick up the bowl of melted ice cream, their wineglasses and the bottle.

Without a look or a word, he headed around the corner toward the back door, leaving her and Hoss, who'd stirred from where he'd plopped beneath her end of the swing, to trail in his wake.

She couldn't blame him for gruffly calling an end to their impromptu make-out session. But it was his very gruffness, his seemingly unmotivated accusations, that led her to suspect he was pushing her away.

It shouldn't surprise her that he was afraid to trust, considering his recent history. She could understand the sentiment.

So why had he kissed her in the first place? Why had he taken their relationship, if she could even call what was between them that, to the level of physical intimacy?

Maybe because he *was* a rescuer. A man who took in abandoned dogs and offered his comfort to damsels in distress.

Damsels who too often had an agenda.

Damsels like her.

When she turned the corner and saw him holding the back screen door open with the toe of his boot, patiently waiting for her, she knew she had to set the record straight once and for all.

As she approached him, his expression guarded, she said, "Just so you know, Mitch, I don't need rescuing."

He waited until she was walking past him through the door to softly reply, "Wouldn't dream of trying, Miss Sullivan."

Chapter Seven

The screen door shut behind Hoss and Mitch with a low, distant rumble that made him pause. Then he realized it was coincidentally timed far-off thunder. He'd been too distracted the last couple of days to take note of the weather forecast. His stomach tightened in the way that all ranchers' did when they had animals exposed on the plains.

His intention had been to escort Alison to the entryway to pick up her purse and see her out to her truck and out of his life. He instead headed for the small black radio he kept on the counter near the stove and switched it on.

With the radio permanently set to a station that ran continuous regional weather and farm reports, he didn't have to wait long for his fears to be confirmed. A storm was heading this way. Wind, lightning and, worst of all, hail. And not just any hail. The crop-crushing, cow-killing sort of hail. The worst possible kind for a man who might need to use his herd to free himself from any and all obligations.

He turned to look at Alison hovering on the other side of the kitchen table as more specific details of the storm were given, such as wind speeds and the storm's predicted trajectory and scope. Her blue-green eyes were wide as if she understood the potential for disaster contained in the weather system heading this way.

But a *town girl* wouldn't have any real clue, wouldn't understand the losses he could sustain from this storm.

He clicked the radio off. "I'm afraid now I *really* have to put an end to this evening." He headed around the table to usher her toward the hall. "I have a bit of scrambling to do before that storm reaches the Circle S."

She stood pulling on her lower lip with her teeth, staring at some spot on the floor.

He extended a hand for her to go first toward the door into the dining room, the shortest route to the front door. He needed her out of his hair so he could get to work.

She didn't budge. Finally, she met his gaze. The intelligence and determination he saw in her eyes never ceased to impress him.

"Those calves you were talking about using to rebuild your herd, if you have to, need to be brought in. The hail could easily kill them."

Her quiet statement of fact surprised him and made him pause in the act of reaching for her elbow. He gave a single nod. "Yes, I do. And yes, it could."

She gave a short, quick nod of her own, pulled out a chair from beneath the table and sat down. Leaning forward, she started yanking one pant leg up. "Where do you keep your extra rain gear and boots?"

He planted his hands on his hips and shifted his weight to one foot impatiently. "The storm is still miles away. You'll have no problem at all getting back to Whiskey Ridge as you are."

She rolled her eyes. "Please." She exposed one slender black-leather-encased lower leg, then unzipped the tall boot.

Not entirely recovered from their make-out session on the porch swing, Mitch's mouth went dry. "What are you doing?" he croaked.

"You don't expect me to help you bring those calves in wearing these things, do you?"

His jaw went slack and his pulse lurched. "I don't expect you to help me bring those calves in at all." Fun and games were over. He needed her gone. His decision to pay back the million dollars was distraction enough.

She pulled the boot from her foot before giving him an exasperated look. "Your men are probably at the festival in town, right?"

Stupidly disappointed that she had a thin black sock on beneath her boot, he yanked his gaze up to hers. What had he expected, fishnet stockings? It wasn't as if she was doing a strip tease for him! He crossed his arms over his chest. "Good chance."

She set the boot down next to her chair and lifted the other leg. "And even if they've heard about the storm, they probably won't get out here in time."

His attention drifted down to what her hands were doing again. She had nice ankles. "Carl wouldn't need to hear any weather report. He'd know just by the way his joints feel. Only positive thing to come out of his rodeo days." Was it his imagination, or were her movements slower, more deliberate?

Another black boot slid away. "Unless that new bride of his managed to get him out on the dance floor, like you said she'd planned on doing. He'll probably blame any aches and pains on dancing." She shook her head and heaved a resigned sigh. "You're going to need my help."

Mitch turned on his heel and went to get his silver metal thermos from the cupboard. "Put your boots back on, Miss Sullivan. I don't need your help."

"You can't go out there by yourself."

He poured into the thermos the coffee they hadn't gotten around to drinking thanks to that little chocolate sauce incident out on the porch swing. He would have been better off handing her dessert on a paper plate and shepherding her out the door. "I can, and I will."

"Well, if you lose those calves, maybe you'll reconsider mortgaging everything to the hilt."

He turned to look at her. Her interest was focused on the three-inch, stiletto heel of her left boot. She was trying to play it cool, but the hope had been clear in her voice.

The idea that she cared about what happened to his ranch rattled the cage he was trying to keep his emotional and physical attraction to her locked in.

Luckily, the bars held firm. "Not a chance, Miss Sullivan."

She looked him in the eye. "You can't suddenly pretend as if you didn't have your mouth on mine, Mitch. Don't insult me by going back to calling me Miss Sullivan."

Mentally wincing, he ran a hand over his face. "You're right, Alison. I apologize." For being an idiot in all sorts of ways.

"Now, let me help you. I promise not to expect anything in return."

He continued to hesitate, certain it was dangerous to allow her to stay because of who she'd been employed by and the questionable strength of his resistance to her.

She dropped the black boot to the floor with a dull thunk and added, "Those calves don't deserve to get pummeled because of your stubbornness."

He released a noisy breath. She was right. The risk of losing the calves was greater than the risk of having her around. And two people would be able to drive them to shelter faster and more effectively than one.

Hopefully she wouldn't prove more of a hindrance than a help.

Grabbing the thermos cup from the cupboard—he normally didn't bother with it—he stuffed a cork in his worry about Alison once and for all. "I'm pretty sure there's an extra set of rain gear in the closet beneath the stairs. You should grab one of my jackets, too. Unless you've got one in your truck. The temp's going to drop big time."

She shot to her feet. "Thanks. Boots?"

"There should be a pair of barn boots in that bin on the porch." He glanced down at the thin black socks covering her slender feet. A hint of appropriate red polish could be seen on her toes. She sure was a fire-cracker from stem to stern. "I'll get you a thick pair of socks to keep your feet from freezing and to help take up the excess space, but you'll still have to be careful that you don't walk out of the boots. My feet are a hell of a lot bigger than yours."

She smiled crookedly. "It'd be scary if they weren't. Don't worry, I'll be fine." She hustled out of the kitchen into the hall.

Praying she was right, he screwed the cup onto the top of the thermos and set it on the table on his way to the dryer in the laundry nook to dig out a pair of clean wool socks.

By the time he returned with some, Alison was back in the kitchen, tugging the bright yellow rain-pants' suspenders higher beneath his quilted red flannel shirt-jacket. She had a yellow slicker and his fleece-lined jeans jacket slung across her other arm. "Horse or ATV?"

Mitch blinked at her efficiency and thoughtfulness for a second before asking, "You know how to ride either?" She might be on her way down the road, after all, if she didn't.

She tossed him the jeans jacket. "Enough to manage."

He grunted and pulled on his jacket. Hopefully enough to manage not getting killed. "ATV. Faster and less risky."

She gave a quick nod of agreement and, with her jaw set in an all-business way, came to get the socks from him.

He made sure the stove was off and grabbed the thermos from the table. "There's a big hay shed near where the cows and their calves should be."

He pushed the screen door open for her, then once they were both through, closed the back door so Hoss wouldn't try to follow them. The old guy was nothing if not game. But like Mitch's other companion that evening, Hoss didn't always know what was good for him.

Mitch continued, "I separated them from the rest of my herd to minimize exposure to disease. They should all fit in under the cover, so we only have to get them as far as the shed."

They went to the bin where he kept his work boots. He set the thermos down on the porch and dug out a pair of rubber barn boots. He handed them to her, then grabbed his work boots and sat down on the edge of the bin to change out of the clean pair he'd worn for dinner.

It'd been a long time since he'd even thought about which boots he had on for a woman, but he could easily blame Alison's choice of foot gear for his keeping-up-with-the-Joneses behavior. Those high-heel boots of hers had certainly made an impression on him. Thus far she'd lived up to the "bring it on" message they sent.

Alison made quick work of donning his thicker socks—though he probably should find yet another pair for her to shove down into the toe of the boot to take up the extra space. But she had the boots on lickety-split, too, so he stomped his way into his own boots, grabbed the thermos and headed for the edge of the porch closest to the equipment barn.

The large halogen light mounted above the barn doors was on a timer and had just clicked on, providing plenty of light for them to see to cross the yard.

"What about all this?"

Mitch turned to see Alison pointing at the table, still sporting part of their meal and place settings. At some point the wind had extinguished the candles despite their protective votives.

He was about to say forget about it when she grabbed the corners of the tablecloth, gathered them together and lifted the resulting bundle off the table with only a few minor *clanks*.

She winced at the sound of glass coming together and started for the kitchen door. "If anything turns up broken, it'll give your sisters another reason to go shopping at Pottery Barn. I'll send them a gift certificate."

Mitch laughed. "They'll love you for that."

Damn, but she kept giving him reasons to like her. More than he wanted to. He found it hard to resist such a go-to kind of gal.

More clanking and an "oops" came from the kitchen, then Alison was hustling back out, closing the door in her wake with a farewell to the dog.

A faint flash of lightning off in the distance caught his attention, and he didn't wait for the rumble of thunder or Alison to reach him before he turned and strode to the long metal outbuilding that housed his truck and equipment. The silver thermos tucked beneath his arm, he buttoned his coat, thankful Alison had grabbed it for him. The temperature had dropped significantly as he'd predicted.

Alison caught up to him as he was pushing one of the big sliding doors open. Without being asked, she put her shoulder into the other one and got it moving along its track and out of the way. Mitch couldn't find fault in her enthusiasm.

Nonetheless, he vowed right then and there to leave her behind if she ran into trouble driving the ATV. He could always pick her up on his way back after he had the calves safe.

He flicked on the lights inside the building and went around his truck to get to the side bay where the four-wheel, all-terrain vehicles were kept. Fate had certainly made it possible for Alison to accompany him tonight. If Carl hadn't abandoned him when she'd showed up while they were working on the fence, the second ATV wouldn't have been repaired yet.

Mitch placed the thermos in the storage box mounted on the back of his ATV, then checked to make sure both had full gas tanks. They did—again, thanks to Carl—so he tossed Alison the smaller, bright red helmet he kept on hand for his sisters.

Sadly, their days of roaring along the fence lines with him had passed. Megan's dentist fiancé frowned on her wilder ways, and Michelle was too busy with her post-graduate work.

Alison caught the helmet easily. "Thanks."

"And you're going to need some gloves." He looked at the shelves on the wall behind the four-wheelers. "Aah—"

"Is it okay if I wear those?"

He turned to find her pointing at a pair of gloves draped over the handlebars of the ATV he'd ridden last. He must have left them there. Normally he was better about putting stuff away properly, but not much had felt normal since she'd showed up with her letter. "Yeah, go ahead."

While she pulled the helmet and gloves on, Mitch retrieved his olive-green rain gear from his truck. By the time he had the bottoms on, she was pushing the red ATV out past him. Another boom of thunder echoed inside the metal barn. This time a heck of a lot closer.

He yanked on the jacket as fast as he could. If the weather service was right and the storm was packing a potentially deadly, icy punch, he and Alison were running out of time.

He hurried to the remaining ATV, slipped on his black helmet and pushed the four-wheeler past his truck and outside. Another roar greeted him, but this time it was Alison starting up her ATV. Though she looked like a little kid sitting on the thing in her too-big rain gear—with only the bridge of her slender nose and her heavily lashed eyes visible above the helmet's jaw shield—she revved the engine with the necessary authority.

A combination of relief and annoyance flooded him. Relief because she *did* know at least something about four-wheelers. She might actually be of some help. Annoyance because it also meant he had one more reason to like and admire her. One more reason to feel bad about preventing her from completing the job she needed to do to get out of debt.

He tore his gaze from her and hardened his jaw.

Not sure how bad the storm might be, he took the time to close the outbuilding's doors before climbing aboard his ATV. He pulled a pair of gloves from his rain slicker's pocket and donned them. After he started the engine, he gave Alison a thumbs-up. She returned the gesture, so he put the four-wheeler into gear and peeled out of the yard.

He took a quick look over his shoulder and wasn't all that surprised to find Alison right on his tail. When he had to make a sharp turn to navigate a fence cut that would head them up the right trail, she handled the maneuver like a pro. She even moved out to the side a bit so her headlight would illuminate more of the ground ahead for him, as well. She hadn't exaggerated her abilities. If anything, she'd minimized them. Why in the world would she want to do that?

The left front wheel of his ATV glanced off a rock on the edge of the trail and nearly jerked the handlebar out of his grip. A reminder he needed to keep his attention on what he was doing if he wanted to reach the cattle he might be staking his future on in one piece.

They passed the two-story-tall hay shed, really nothing more than a roof on stilts. He noted with relief that enough of the hay had been used during the winter to allow space beneath the cover for the cows and their calves, but not so much as to rob them of protection. If he needed to, he could pull down a few bales to build an additional wall, depending on which way the wind came at them.

A fence line separated the grazing area the calves had been taken to from the close-in acreage, and Mitch had to open a gate that would allow them through. Alison waited patiently somewhere inside the too-big yellow rain gear for him to get the gate open and fastened back, then lead the way through.

The cold wind had picked up with telling speed by the time they reached the good grazing land where he'd pastured the small herd of his best breeders and their calves. Mitch knew it wouldn't be long before the rain and whatever else might be in store for them started to fall. He blew out a relieved breath when he spotted the cattle bunched together not far from the trail.

The calves, most a good four months from being ready to wean, had tucked up tight to the cows to stay warm. The cows simply looked at the two noisy intruders with flat, glowing eyes from where they lay or stood guard. Mitch stopped a good distance from them and let his engine idle. Alison pulled up right next to him.

He leaned toward her, pulling the face guard on his helmet down so she'd be able to hear him shout,

"They're used to the sound of the ATVs, but the headlights might spook them, so don't get too close. Plus, I picked these cows for insemination because they're good mamas, which means they occasionally get protective of their calves. Keep on your toes."

He made a wide arc with his hand. "We'll circle around behind them to get 'em moving, then you keep them on the trail by riding on the left side, and I'll work the right, okay?"

She nodded and shouted back, "Okay."

Mitch readjusted his helmet and put the ATV into gear. He slowly drove his four-wheeler around the cluster of cattle. Knowing the drill despite it being nighttime, the cows that had been lying down lurched to their feet and the ones standing shuffled their hooves.

He rose up off the seat to see Alison moving slowly into position on the other side, just the right distance away to avoid a charge but still assert some pressure on the cows to move. She did seem to know what she was doing.

Curiosity grew.

Mitch was about to give the sharp, shrill whistle that would set the cattle in motion, but the damn near exact sound came from the left side of the small herd. He blinked. Alison sounded like one of his men working the cattle. How had a town girl learned to do that?

His speculation was cut off when a torrent of rain was unleashed with no preamble at all, like a giant tap in the sky being turned on full blast. Thanks to a gap between the collar of his slicker and his helmet, water ran in icy rivulets down his neck, chilling him to the bone.

The cattle wanted to turn their rumps to the weather and cluster together, but with the combined whistles and urging from him and Alison, they were able to keep the herd moving in the direction of the shelter.

The rain beat a deafening rhythm on his helmet and nearly blinded him. He was pretty sure that Alison had a decent visor on the helmet he'd given her. At least he hoped she did.

Either way, she probably regretted her insistence to help him out by now.

He didn't. Yeah, he could have moved the herd himself, but it would have taken a hell of a lot longer and been more difficult.

Mitch could see her headlight bouncing as she rode over the rougher ground next to the trail they were keeping the cattle on, but he only caught occasional glimpses of her sitting tall on the four-wheeler. His admiration-ometer dinged as she maxed it out. She really was something. Thank goodness she wasn't country born and bred or he'd have a hard time resisting her, regardless of why she'd showed up on his ranch.

They were almost to the hay shed when the smacking of the rain became an ominous pinging on his helmet and the broad metal fenders of the ATV.

The rain was turning to hail.

He wouldn't have had time to go it alone. Gratitude

toward the woman who'd turned his life upside down heated him from the chest out.

The pings turned to bangs as the hail grew in size.

The calves started to bleat.

Mitch revved the engine and moved in closer to force the cows to pick up their pace, but the blowing hail and the darkness made them reluctant. To keep the herd moving, he occasional popped the clutch to lurch the four-wheeler at the lollygaggers.

Finally, the steeply pitched, corrugated metal roof protecting the stacked bails of hay flashed in his headlight. Whether motivated by the smell of easy food or the good sense to seek shelter, the cows broke into eager trots that forced the calves to gallop to keep as close to their mamas as possible. They worked their way through the gate, then headed straight for the protected hay.

Mitch had to roar up to a couple of the lead cows who wanted to stand and eat the hay from the outside rather than from under the shelter of the roof, but they were easy enough to convince to get out of the hail growing bigger and coming down harder by the second. Alison was busy easing the last of the cows and their calves under the large cover.

None too soon. Mitch had just pulled beneath the cover and cut his engine—leaving the headlight on—when hail the size of baseballs started coming down with the kind of force Major League pitchers dream about. When he heard Alison cut her engine, yet saw the light shining on the back of the herd, he blew out a heart-calming breath of relief. He sat back, working his sopping wet gloves from his hands.

Mitch barely caught the sound of Alison's exclamation of pain over the escalating clamor of hail on the metal roof. Fear blazed through him.

He stood up on the footplates to see over the big animals. Alison wasn't under the cover yet and was getting pummeled by the huge, round chunks of ice. The cattle hadn't moved far enough forward under the shelter to make room for her to drive in, but she'd turned off her engine, anyway. The fool woman!

Yanking off his helmet, Mitch yelled, "Alison, get in! Forget the ATV! Get the hell in!"

Her shoulders hunkered, she leapt off the four-wheeler, but stubborn to a fault, she took the time to try to push it in among the cows under the cover of the metal roof. The hail was bouncing off her helmet with sickening clanks, but it was the thud of the ones hitting her rain slicker that had his heart in his throat.

Mitch jumped off his own ride and ran for her, skirting the edge of the clustered cows, their combined body heat already sending up a musky-smelling steam despite the chill wind. The icy mud was slick beneath his boots, and he almost went down twice, but he had to get to her.

His heart thundered louder in his ears than the roar of hail on metal. When he reached her he grabbed her arm and hauled her farther under the cover, shouldering cows out of their way until she was safe from the crushing, wind-blown deluge.

He bent to find what was visible of her face through the gap in the helmet and yelled to be heard over the din from the hail. "Are you nuts? What were you thinking?"

Her eyes were mere slits and glittered suspiciously in the headlight of her ATV. The thought that she'd been hurt enough to cry tore at his gut. Enough to make him admit that whether he wanted to or not, he cared about her. Here she was, out here helping him salvage his future.

She pulled away from him and bent to remove the helmet from her head. When she straightened with a flip of her long, half-soaked hair, she let out a howl.

Mitch's stomach clenched with a fierceness normally reserved for members of his family. How could he have been so stupid to let her come help him? She talked tough, but she was so feminine.

"Wow!" She grinned widely at him, her straight white teeth flashing, and it dawned on him that the noise she'd made had actually been a whoop of glee. Her eyes weren't glistening with tears, they were sparkling with pleasure.

She gave him a playful shove. "Man, was that close, or what! But we did it! We got them under just in time." She whooped again. "Talk about awesome! What a rush!"

Mitch blinked at her. Maybe the helmet hadn't protected her brain from the barrage after all. "You serious?"

She laughed, the sound musical compared with the cacophony of solid ice on sheet metal. "Are you kidding? Of course I'm serious. That was a blast! Thanks for letting me help." She turned to scratch the ear of a calf that had decided the backside of her smooth, plastic-coated rain slicker was worth licking. "I'd forgotten how cute these little guys are."

"You'd *forgotten?*"

Though her cheeks were already red from the cold and the chafing of the helmet she'd tucked under her arm, he could have sworn she blushed. "Uh—"

Suddenly everything that had happened in the last hour made sense. The practiced efficiency, the skill on the four-wheeler, the knowledge of herding, the *whistle.* "Wait a minute." He raised an accusing finger at her. "You're not a town girl, after all. You were raised on a *ranch,* weren't you?"

Chapter Eight

Alison opened her mouth, fully intending to lie to Mitch about where she'd grown up. But he'd been lied to so much already in his life, she couldn't bring herself to do it. Not over something that only mattered to her.

She snapped her mouth shut again.

He leveled a finger at her nose. "You knew exactly what to do the whole time and you did it perfectly. And that whistle! Only someone who's been around live-stock whistles like you did."

Pleasure bubbled up in her from his praise. Unable to suppress a grin, she dropped her chin and pulled the soaking wet gloves off. "Oh, I don't know about that. I'd say there are more than a few construction workers out there who come pretty close...."

He actually harrumphed and crossed his arms over the front of his rain slicker.

Adrenaline and sorely missed happiness made her dang near giddy. She laughed and went up on tiptoes momentarily so he'd hear her. "I'm sorry, but you really look like a grumpy old-man-of-the-sea with your oil-stained rain gear and your hair all goofy from your helmet."

He scowled harder. "And you're avoiding the subject. Were you raised on a ranch, or not?"

She sighed and pushed the wet ends of her hair off her face. "A farm, actually. My dad grows several different types of crops, but he's also always kept a small herd of cattle. Herefords. I used to help him with them." Her dear father had seen what she was capable of on the farm, but for some reason he'd assumed that in the outside world, she'd be as helpless and vulnerable as Mitch's calves. Scott had been a whole lot meaner in his final assessments.

She watched Mitch chew on the information for a moment, his sharp gaze traveling over her face in a way that would have made her want to squirm if she wasn't having such a good time. He was clearly trying to decide whether or not to believe her. She couldn't blame him for being suspicious.

Her heart gave that funny little squeeze it did every time she thought about what he'd had dumped at his feet. Didn't help that she'd been the "dumper."

Finally he uncrossed his arms, only to plant his fists on his hips. "Never would have guessed it from your urban-chic routine."

That brought her chin up. "It's not a routine. It's for real. Who I am now. I've had my fill of rural life, thank you very much. I'm a town girl, through and through. Never going back." To do so would be an admission that she didn't have what it took to make it in the real world. She did, and she would.

"It shows." A mocking smile played at the corners of his sensual mouth as he nodded at the hand she'd unconsciously offered to the calf to lick instead of her filthy rain gear.

She snatched her hand away and tucked it behind her back. Deprived of its make-do salt lick, the calf proceeded to butt her, knocking her sideways a step. She shoved it away toward its mother.

Mitch gave her a speculative look. "So everything you were saying about Dependable was nothing more than a song and dance. You didn't really grow up there."

The calf, more interested in something salty than milky, jostled her again. She relented and let it lick her palm once more with its warm, raspy tongue. Unable to resist the velvety spot between the baby's eyes anymore now than she'd been able to as a kid, she stroked it with the knuckles on her other hand.

She kept her chin high when she looked back at Mitch. "I've never given you any 'song and dance.' Dependable was the closest town to our farm, and I went as often as I could. Dependable, and the McCoys, are everything I said they were. And more." A list of positives started forming in her head, much the way it had on the day she'd rented the bullhorn.

He waved away her assertion. "Okay, fine. As far as I'm concerned, that topic remains off-limits—"

She interrupted, "Not as far as *I'm* concerned—"

"Alison, please." Despite his word choice, there was no pleading in his tone. His gaze strayed to what she was doing with her hands and his brows rose.

She shrugged at being caught petting the calf while it licked her. "My hands are cold and the gloves are soaked."

Her excuse sent him into action. "Among other things, I'm sure. Come here." He reached for her and quickly wrapped an arm around her shoulder.

The contact sent pain shooting through her from numerous spots. She winced and tried to shy away. She knew she'd taken some pretty good hits from the hail on her shoulders, arms and back, but the rush of adrenaline must have kept her from noticing more than the initial pain. But she definitely noticed it now. Each and every spot stung like crazy.

He jerked his arm upward off her shoulders. "Dammit, I knew you were getting hurt. Come on back against the hay. These beefy bodies will block the wind." He took the hand she'd been petting the calf with, his grip gentle but firm, and led the way through the two dozen or so coal-black cows and their calves.

The simple touch of his hand sent a thrill through her, a thrill as irrationally potent as his caress had been earlier that evening on the porch swing. And now there was an added element of possessiveness. No, it was a protectiveness, the impression strengthened by the way he pulled her close to his big body whenever a cow shifted as if she might kick.

Scott had never conveyed that level of caring. She shook her head at her thought that Mitch cared about her. The crazy events of the night must be making her delirious. He was just waiting until he could get rid of her.

Alison realized the hail wasn't falling as intensely when she was able to hear Mitch's deep voice, soft and coaxing, as he reassured the big animals. When necessary he pushed the cattle gently aside so the two of them could make their way toward what was left of the stack of winter feed.

She struggled against the effect his voice had on her. Getting emotional would keep her from doing her job, from securing her independence once and for all.

The cows that had reached the cover first had settled in to chewing happily on the partial wall of oversize bales stair-stepped upward. Their oh-so-attractive mud and manure spattered rumps formed an impressive wall of their own.

"Make way, ladies." Mitch pushed a couple of already well-fed cows aside with his free hand, then pulled Alison forward. He directed her to the lowest bale that had others stacked higher on two sides. "Wedge yourself back in the corner there."

Alison complied, fighting with everything in her not to grimace. Without the warming exertion of steering the four-wheeler over rough ground and the excitement of getting the herd under the shelter distracting her, she hurt more than she cared to admit.

Her slow, deliberate movements must have given her away because Mitch growled and cursed softly. He left her and made his way to the side of the shed where he'd left his ATV.

Just as the lack of pulsing adrenaline allowed her to feel the pain where she'd been hit by the hail, the lack of Mitch's proximity allowed the cold bite of the wind to seep all the way into her muscles. Her body responded by tightening into uncontrollable shivering. After clenching her molars together to stop her teeth from chattering, she heard the snap of the storage box mounted behind the seat of Mitch's ATV and saw the light from a heavy-duty flashlight glistening off the wet cattle.

Not sure how long the dangerous part of the storm might linger over them, she unclenched her teeth long enough to yell, "You might want to turn off the headlights to save the ATV batteries!"

"They'll be fine. We're not going to have to hole up here for that long."

As if to make a liar out of him, the hail surged again, sounding like a train rumbling overhead. Several of the calves bleated in fear.

The headlight on his ATV went out.

She smiled. At least the man was willing to acknowledge she was right about one thing.

The flashlight he'd brought out was large, yet its

beam didn't rival the size of the headlight. Thankfully the other ATV's headlight was still strong enough to reach them from the other end of the shed. But who knew how long that battery would last?

Mitch made his way back and she saw he'd also brought the thermos of hot coffee with him. Alison moaned in anticipation.

She reached for the silver thermos as soon as he drew near enough. "Oh, you are a wonderful man."

He snorted and joined her on the bale. Settling on his knees at her side with the flashlight shining on her, he said. "You're probably right about saving the juice in at least one of the ATV batteries. Hailstorms this intense usually don't last all that long, but we're better safe than sorry."

As she worked to make her numb hands unscrew the thermos, she nodded at the other headlight backlighting the steaming cows and their calves. "What about the other one?"

"If it croaks, we can always double up on mine to get back."

The image of fitting herself snugly up against Mitch, her arms wrapped around his trim waist, her breasts pressed against his strong back, warmed her up some. It also distracted her enough that she didn't notice he'd taken the thermos from her until the heavenly scent of hot, strong black coffee replaced the pungent combination of cattle, mud and hay.

He half filled the cup he'd removed and handed it to her.

About to gripe about his stinginess with the coffee, she stopped herself when the wildly dancing hot liquid made her realize how hard she'd been shivering. She directed a grateful smile up at him. "Wonderful *and* smart."

"Just experienced," he said, dismissing her praise. "Drink that as best you can." He took a drink himself straight from the thermos.

She could already feel the heat from the coffee seeping through the metal cup to her hands. Raising it slowly, she took a few tentative sips to keep from burning her mouth, but the heat of the coffee felt so good on its way to her stomach she decided she didn't care about a little scalding. She took a big drink and grimaced at the strong, bitter taste.

He chuckled knowingly. "Cowboy brew."

"I thought that was a myth."

"Does it taste like a myth?" he asked as he set the thermos aside.

She laughed, then took another shiver-calming drink. "Well, it sure as heck doesn't taste like a hazelnut latte, either, but I'll survive."

"I'm glad," he said solemnly, and leaned toward her.

She stopped shivering altogether. It hadn't been that long ago when all she'd been aware of was the heat generated between them.

Reaching for the upturned collar of her yellow rain slicker, he murmured, "Let's open this thing up and check you out." He pulled open the first snap closure.

Not sure how to handle his concern or her awareness of him, she held her cup out of the way and joked, "You planning on killing time with a literal roll in the hay?"

He stilled.

If only she could see his face. She silently scoffed at herself. As if being able to tell what he was thinking would help her know how to react. Or give her the ability to handle her own body's enthusiasm for the off-handed suggestion. Talk about a Freudian slip.

After a drawn-out moment that left her breathless, he moved again. "Interesting thought, but I can't say I'm that crass. You're hurt and freezing. Let me have a look at what those hailstones—make that hail *boulders*—did to you."

The sight of his big hands gently parting the rain coat and quilted flannel shirt over her black T-shirt-clad breasts was hypnotic. "I'm fine. Just a little banged up."

"I've know hail that size to break a man's collarbone."

"Then it's a good thing I'm not a man."

He snorted a laugh but continued with what he was doing. He touched his fingers to said bone, probing with the barest pressure.

Though his hands were nowhere near as warm as they had been when he'd slipped one beneath her shirt on the porch swing and his interest now was supposedly clinical, there was enough of a trailing caress in his touch that her breathing turned fast and shallow. She looked like a steam engine, her breath huffing out of her in white puffs in the cold air.

She barely noticed the thundering hail tapering off to a hard downpour of rain.

"Nothing's broken, Mitch, I swear." Good thing she no longer needed to shout to be heard, because she doubted she could muster the volume thanks to his breath-stealing attention.

He ran his hands under the slicker to her shoulders. He hit a sore spot and she gritted her teeth to keep from flinching. He noticed and instantly lifted his hands off her, easing them from under her coat.

Sitting back on his heels, he shook his head. "I was an idiot for letting you come with me."

"How can you say that? You saw how close we cut it. If you hadn't had my help driving the herd along you would have never gotten them under cover in time." She nodded at the cattle. "Those calves didn't have the benefit of a motorcycle helmet like I did. There's absolutely no doubt you would have lost at least some of them."

A thought occurred to her. "Where is the rest of your herd? Are they going to get hit, too?"

Propping himself with a hand, he shifted his legs out from under him and sat down next to her. It had to be her imagination, with two layers of heavy plastic between them, but she swore she could feel the heat generated by his big body.

Once settled, shoulder to shoulder with her, he answered, "Most of them are south of here. I'm pretty sure the hail missed them, judging by how the storm appeared to be tracking. But I am running some steers east of the house. I'll send one of the guys to check on them tomorrow while the rest of us track down the main herd."

Alison chafed at the fact that he had yet another excuse—this time a good one—for not going to Dependable with her anytime soon. With the subject "off-limits," she was pretty much left high and dry.

And soon to be a colossal failure.

One that was hurting in all sorts of ways. Despite the warmth coming off Mitch and from the coffee, the cold had gained a tight hold on her muscles, and the spots where she'd been hit by the monster hail throbbed horribly.

She closed her eyes against the pain, willing her body to relax.

"You don't have to pretend to be so tough, you know."

Alison jerked her eyes open and turned to look at him. He was watching her, the upward curve of his mouth gentled by understanding. Something very close to admiration softened his gaze.

A trick of the deep shadows.

The same shadows that lent intimacy to the moment.

His protective closeness lulled her, made her feel safe. It seemed only right to answer truthfully. She didn't have much to lose. "Yes I do. It's my only defense at this point."

"Defense against what, Alison?"

Against the failure my ex-husband predicted for me and that my father expected. Against the loss of every dream I've ever had. Against my burgeoning feelings for you.

Praying he couldn't see the truth in her face, she

quirked her mouth and quipped, "Against the big, bad world, that's what."

"The world's not all bad, you know."

She looked out at the wall of rain sparkling like a beaded curtain in the spotlight. "It can be when things aren't going your way."

He sat silent next to her, but she could feel his struggle. Whether against pity or resolve, she didn't know. She chose not to look to see if she could tell. She didn't want his pity and she already knew he was the sort of man who stuck to his resolve.

He carefully slipped an arm around her shoulders.

So it was pity. Her battered pride shuddered and nearly caved in response. Sheer stubbornness kept the walls holding her together intact and the hurt hidden.

The minute he settled the weight of his hand on the top of her arm, pain exploded beneath his touch and she hissed through her teeth.

"I'm sorry!" He snatched his hand away. "That's it. I need to get you home. I think the part of the storm packing the dangerous punch has passed. We can make it back without being beaten to death. Time to get you back to the house and checked out properly."

She raised the shield of humor and an eyebrow in a look of mock indignation. "You seriously need to work on your pick-up lines, Mr. Smith."

He moved the thermos and flashlight and scooted off the bale of hay. "I have yet to find the need for pick-up lines, Miss Sullivan."

She groused, "No doubt." He probably had woman popping up from the sagebrush wanting to be with him.

He held his hands out to help her down. A simple, caring gesture that for some reason touched her profoundly and brought stinging tears to her eyes.

Preferring he saw physical weakness rather than emotional frailty, she screwed up her face in a grimace. As she grabbed his hands she added, "Because you've that secret sauce thing going."

Apparently too focused on the fact she was in pain, he ignored her comment and pulled his hands out of hers. "Here, let me lift you off."

Before she could protest he fit his hands in her armpits—the one place guaranteed not to have been hit by hailstones—and lifted her off the hay bale in one smooth motion.

His gentle strength took her breath away. She could only stare up at him as he set her on her feet directly in front of him. He was so handsome and funny and steadfast and caring. She hadn't believed that guys like him really existed anymore.

"You okay?" he asked, his hands lingering on her.

Unexpected longing for a man like him in her life tightened her throat so much she could barely swallow, let alone talk. After a moment she managed a "yeah."

His thumbs moved along the plastic rain slicker on the sides of her breasts and his gaze drifted to her mouth.

Suddenly Alison wasn't cold anymore. Just the opposite. The memory of being in his arms, of what his touch and kiss felt like, heated her more effectively than a dip in hot water. Muscles that had been seized tight and shuddering in self-defense became languid with a sensual warmth.

For the second time that night, nothing else mattered but the incredible way he made her feel. Wanted.

Mitch's face drew closer and she closed her eyes in anticipation. His lips hadn't touched hers, but she already knew his kiss was a balm for every bruise she'd ever suffered on the inside. And she didn't care if it could only be temporary.

Something besides her abandoned resistance shoved her sideways.

She cried out in surprise. Mitch reacted swiftly, tightening his hold on her, pulling her against him and turning to protect her with his body.

They both looked back and found a calf staring expectantly at them. It raised its moist, leathery nose and sniffed, then edged around Mitch to lick Alison's yellow raincoat. If she wasn't mistaken, it was the same calf she'd let lick her hand earlier.

She laughed and scratched the black tuft between the calf's big ears. "Little stinkpot."

Mitch dipped his head to the side to look at the calf's belly. "Just what I suspected. A bull." He straightened and shook his head with mock seriousness. "Some guys aren't content with only one taste. Next thing you know, they're coming back for more."

Needing to regain some control, she met his gaze and

said daringly, "That can be a good thing if it's done in the right way." Maybe keeping their interaction superficial would provide a semblance of protection against his effect on her.

He pushed her helmet-flattened hair away from her face while a seriousness settled in the lines bracketing his mouth. "You're better off sending them on their way." He stepped past her and shooed the calf back toward the open end of the covered area.

Not sure if he was chastising himself or her—or speaking from personal experience—Alison kept quiet.

Mitch turned to her with a critical eye. "I think you'd better ride back with me."

She ignored all the throbbing welts she could feel swelling up and straightened. "I'm fine. You won't want to waste time tomorrow coming back out here for the other ATV. Plus, I'm assuming you're not planning on leaving this bunch here to gorge themselves on all this hay?"

He created a cloud in front of him when his heavy sigh hit the cold air. "No. They need to go back to the other side of the fence." He snagged the handles of the big flashlight and the thermos with one hand and pointed to the ground at her feet with the other. "You stay put while I get them through the gate."

Without waiting for her to agree or disagree with his command, he made his way through the cattle to his ATV, pushing and whistling to start the animals moving away from the hay.

Alison ignored his command on principle alone. She waited until he had put the flashlight and thermos back into the ATV's storage box and was pulling his helmet on before she headed toward the blinding headlight of the ATV she'd ridden. The loud rev of Mitch's four-wheeler coming to life trumped the noise of the heavy rain on the metal roof, but the addition of another headlight to cut the inky darkness was welcome.

As quickly as her sore arms and shoulders allowed, she donned her helmet and freezing, sopping-wet gloves. She clenched her teeth against the pain and cold, then climbed aboard her ATV and started it up. The engine growled loud and long as she held the clutch in and twisted the accelerator. Good. The headlight hadn't drained the battery as she'd feared it would. Her dad's old three-wheeler was far less reliable.

The cattle started to complain and shuffle from beneath the protective roof as she inched her way behind them in a wide turn. More cows and calves trotted past her. The reason why came roaring up next to her.

Mitch brought his ATV to a sliding stop in the hay-strewn mud just ahead of her. "I told you to stay put!"

She stood on the footplates and leaned forward, pulling her chin guard down so he'd be sure to hear her. "When I start a job, I finish it!"

He glared at her for a moment. At least, she assumed he was glaring, because she couldn't really make out his face with a wall of rain between them. Then he saluted and roared away. He curved back around to encourage the rest of the cattle to head back toward their grazing area.

The powerful pleasure he so easily flooded her with made her smile. She watched him for a moment before slowly driving up next to the lead cows to keep them from doubling back toward the shed.

At least the guy had learned when it was pointless arguing with her. Too bad she was also learning the same about him.

Her smile faded as the pleasure dimmed. Things sure as heck weren't going as planned.

She pressed her lips into a determined line.

Regardless of having had more fun than she'd had in ages, she *would* finish this job.

MITCH'S APPRECIATION FOR Alison Sullivan grew as he watched her deftly maneuver the cattle up ahead of him to the gate. The Angus worked their way through the opening with far less enthusiasm than they'd shown the first time, their heads low against the steady rain and the late hour. But between the pressure he was exerting in the back and she on the side, the small herd was slowly making its way back to the prime grazing acreage where he wanted them.

His gaze sought out Alison, or at least the beam of her headlight, yet again. They made a surprisingly good team, the two of them.

Exactly what he'd always wanted from the woman in his life.

His ATV jumped forward unexpectedly when he inadvertently released the clutch. Such a thought entering his head while thinking about Alison made him limp with astonishment. This was the woman he'd wanted gone for good mere hours ago. It was as if he'd been the one who'd been pounded on the head with gigantic hailstones.

Instead he'd simply learned more about her. About both her past and the measure of her grit. He'd found no fault with either. Just the opposite.

The last cows and their calves were ambling toward the opening, and Alison headed for the fastened-back gate. Fearing she'd be stubborn enough to try to heft the gate closed despite her injuries, Mitch put his ride back in gear and zoomed over to the side she was on. He blasted past her and reached the fence before she could. She immediately turned and headed to where he'd been to assure the stragglers did indeed follow the rest of the herd through.

Yep, a surprisingly good team.

He grinned as he cut the engine and vaulted off the four-wheeler to run to the metal gate, secured open against the fence. He unfastened it, and as soon as she urged the last cow and calf through the opening, he hauled the gate away from the fence. The deep, cattle-churned mud grabbed and sucked at his boots and the wind pushed the gate in the opposite direction he wanted it to go, but he put his back into it and got the gate latched closed.

Mitch slogged through the muck to where she waited on her idling ATV. He pulled his helmet down a little so his mouth wasn't totally blocked. "Great job."

She didn't raise her head much or say anything in return. He realized she looked smaller, more hunkered down.

Worry spurted hot into his stomach. "You okay?"

Her helmet waggled up and down.

Maybe there *was* a limit to her toughness. "Let's get back ASAP."

"S-sounds good," she finally answered through chattering teeth.

The muscles in Mitch's chest tightened. He put a gloved hand on her helmet and leaned close. "Why don't you scoot forward and let me drive."

She shook her head, her helmet moving with conviction beneath the palm of his glove. "No. I'd rather we s-stop talking and j-just go." She revved the engine of her ATV in punctuation, then let the clutch up enough that she moved forward and out from under his hand.

He had to laugh and ran splashing back to his ride as quickly as he could in the deep mud. Dang, he liked her. He climbed on his ATV and started it up. Alison reminded him a lot of himself. Stubborn and independent.

Too bad they were ultimately on opposite sides of the proverbial fence. One he personally had no intention of jumping, no matter how green the pasture she wanted him to visit had been made by money. McCoy money. With McCoy strings attached. He'd bet his life on it.

He led the way as fast as he dared in the heavy rain, and found it very telling that she lagged behind his tail on the dirt track instead of riding beside him over rougher terrain. She *was* hurting. The tightness in his chest worsened and his stomach joined in the act. He'd never been so happy to see the lights of his house and outbuildings when they finally appeared in the distance.

To keep from wasting a second at her expense, he drove straight for the back of the house instead of the equipment barn. The ATVs could spend a night in the rain. Getting Alison warm and comfortable ranked a heck of a lot higher on his priority scale.

Sure, he knew she still had an agenda, but she'd done far more than she needed to help him out, and she deserved his care. It was the least he could do for her. And he happened to know the best remedy for a cold, miserable night spent herding cattle.

His four-wheeler had barely stopped before he was off it and hustling to the hot tub at the edge of the porch to haul off the cover and crank the heat. He removed his helmet and headed back to where she'd parked her ATV behind his.

She was watching him as she reached up to take off her helmet with telling slowness. He tucked his under his arm and removed her helmet for her.

Blinking up at him in the rain, she asked, "Haven't you had enough of water tonight?"

He urged her off the ATV and steered her onto the covered porch. "I need to get you warmed up, Alison, and I don't think a pelting shower would feel all that great on your sore spots. Not to mention how your muscles are going to feel after spending that much time jockeying a four-wheeler through muck."

She looked down at herself and let out a chattering laugh. "I think I've brought more than a little of that muck back with me. I'll turn your hot tub into a mud puddle."

"Only if you wear that rain gear in." He set the helmets on the boot bin, peeled his soaked gloves off, and reached for her hand.

Blue-green eyes widened at him. "And what exactly am I supposed to wear?"

An image of Alison skinny-dipping in his hot tub turned his own jets on, but his gaze snagged on her blue-tinged lips and wiped away any and all erotic thoughts. "Come on, let's get you warmed up."

As soon as she realized he intended to haul her straight into the kitchen, she set her rubber boot heels and pulled back. "We can't go inside like this! We're filthy."

Mitch tugged her inside, where they were briefly greeted by Hoss before the dog went back to his bed. "This is a ranch, Alison. The kitchen floor can stand a little mud." He looked down at his own rain pants and coat, now more the same solid brown that her once yellow gear was. "Well, okay, a lot of mud. But I happen to know how to wield a mean mop." He set to unsnapping her jacket, very aware of her attention on his face.

"Is there anything you don't know how to do, Mitch Smith?"

Her softly spoken question brought his eyes back up to hers. There was something there—a yearning, maybe—that set his heart to pounding and stirred a kindred something deep in his noisy chest. "There are lots of things I don't know how to do, Alison Sullivan."

Like how in the hell he was going to send this woman he admired and flat-out cared about more than was good for him on her way without what she came for.

Him.

Chapter Nine

"Like trust?"

When his pupils flared and his gaze searched hers, Alison knew as well as she knew the contents of her own painfully similar emotional baggage that Mitch Smith no longer knew how to trust. Her heart felt like it'd taken a direct hit from the mother of all hailstones.

She ached for him.

"I trust this land, Alison. If I do right by it, it will do right by me."

If only she had something so concrete to cling to, to stake her dreams and future on. Tears pricked the backs of her eyes. She tore her gaze from his and made a grand show of inspecting her mud-splattered sleeve. "I'm afraid I've brought more than a little of your land into your kitchen."

He chuckled and started to peel the muddy raincoat and the flannel shirt-jacket from her. "That's okay. You earned the right."

The respect in his tone brought her gaze back to his.

There was honest appreciation there, enough to melt her ice-encased sense of hope. No matter how this all turned out, she would hold tight to the memory of that look.

Mitch hissed out a breath and brought her thoughts back from fantasy land. "Damn it, Alison, you've been beat to hell."

She looked to where his attention lay on her arms as he gingerly slid the jackets off her. Welts darn near the size of the hailstones that had caused them peppered her skin below her black T-shirt's short sleeves. "Better me than your calves."

He made a grumbling noise as if he didn't exactly agree. "If you weren't so cold already, I'd insist we ice those."

Her back teeth chattered at the mere thought of ice bags. "If you did, I'd have to hurt you."

He tossed the jackets over the back of a kitchen chair and met her gaze with a distinct twinkle in his eyes. "What makes you think I wouldn't like anything you did to me?"

The innuendo in his tone made her shiver for an altogether different reason.

He must have felt it, because his blond brows slammed down and the amusement in his eyes gave way to worry. "I need to get you warm more than I need to treat those welts. Is your underwear decent?"

She choked on a laugh. "Excuse me?"

"Would you be comfortable stripping down to your skivvies to go in the hot tub?"

Automatically, she glanced down at herself and almost gasped at how obviously cold she was. The unlined black satin bra might be infinitely comfortable, but it failed the wet T-shirt test. She jerked her gaze up and caught Mitch staring for a fraction of a second before he brought his attention back up also.

He blinked and turned on his heel. "I'll get you one of my *thick, dark* and *long* T-shirts to wear." He headed for the hall. "You can strip down the rest of the way in the bathroom." Once through the doorway, he pointed to the left as he turned to go right. "It's there."

Alison grinned at his back as he disappeared down the hall. It had been a long time since a man had made her feel this...valued. Both physically and emotionally. And to have that admiration coming from such a great guy...

She sighed as welcomed warmth spread from her chest outward. She followed him from the kitchen and turned in the direction he'd indicated.

A door at the end of the hall opened to a small, white-and-black-tiled bathroom. She grimaced at the clean floor, knowing it wouldn't remain pristine the moment she dropped her trousers. The yellow rain pants were solid mud all the way up the front and sides from the spray off the ATV tires.

Certainly this place had seen worse and recovered, though, being a ranch house and all. Mitch really could cook, he really cared for his herd, and it was obvious he really could wield a mean mop.

And maybe, just maybe, he could learn to trust *her.*

Everyone needed someone to trust. No matter what he said, land didn't count. Once he trusted her he might be more willing to go to Dependable with her.

Further warmed by purpose, Alison hooked her thumbs beneath the yellow suspenders holding up the too-big rain pants. She caught sight of herself in the mirror over the pedestal sink and froze in horror. A smattering of mud covered her face from her upper cheeks to her brows, where the helmet hadn't provided coverage. Her hair was a fuzzy mess where it had stayed dry and a stringy mess where it hadn't.

She looked like a bandit having an extremely bad hair day.

The thought made her laugh out loud. Oh yeah, Mitch had really been tempted by *her*.

Shaking her head at her foolishness, she reached for a long length of toilet paper and dampened it enough to wipe the worst of the dirt off her face. She'd leave her hair to the rain.

Once she'd cleaned her face and dumped the wad of muddy toilet paper in the plastic-lined waste basket beneath the sink, she gingerly pulled the suspenders off her shoulders. She still managed to brush a couple of the welts, igniting sparks of pain. Mitch had been right, she had gotten herself all beat up. But it had been so worth it. She couldn't remember the last time she'd felt such a sense of accomplishment. Or had so much fun.

Fun had been missing from her life in a big way for longer than she cared to consider.

She let the filthy rain pants drop to the floor and stepped out of them, noting thankfully there wasn't a mat in front of the white pedestal sink. Her black jeans were only wet from the knees down, but her T-shirt was soaked from where the rain had trickled down inside the loose collar of the slicker and flannel jacket.

A knock sounded on the door.

"Come in."

The door inched open and Mitch's hand shot through, dangling a dark blue T-shirt.

Opening the door wider, she found him standing with his side toward her in swim trunks that hit his knees. A couple of huge towels were slung over his shoulders and his face was averted. She took advantage of that to blatantly check him out.

Not surprisingly, the arm he had outstretched was thick with well-defined muscles, as were his calves. The hair on his legs and lower arms, though dense, was just as golden as the mussed hair on his head. Seeing so much of him went a long way toward warming her up, but his chivalry—or embarrassment—made her grin.

Finally she said, "I'm still dressed."

He looked at her and his face relaxed. "Oh. Well, here." He offered her the shirt. "This should work."

Wondering at his behavior, considering they'd been making out a matter of hours ago, Alison took the T-shirt from him. "Thanks."

"You're welcome." His gaze traveled downward. "Why don't you hand out your clothes as soon as you have them off. I can toss them in the wash so they'll at least be clean." He held out his other hand to her and she finally noticed he had a folded something made out of gray cotton in his fist. "You can change into these sweats when we're done in the tub and wear them back to your hotel."

Touched by his thoughtfulness, she took the sweats, too. "Thank you."

He shrugged endearingly.

Alison eased the bathroom door closed again and set about getting undressed. Hot man in the hall or not, she was bone cold. Not a good thing. With a grunt of pain, she pulled the black cotton shirt over her head and draped it on the sink.

"Alison?" Mitch's voice came through the door, his concern obvious. He really was a heck of a guy.

"I'm fine." And suddenly very self-conscious about stripping down to the skin with Hot Man in the hall. "Why don't you go ahead and get in the tub. I can handle getting my clothes in the wash."

"I'll wait."

Great.

Having always preferred taking her medicine in one gulp, Alison stripped off her bra, jeans and socks and wadded them up with her shirt on the sink. She couldn't bring herself to go without her black panties under his T-shirt. She would just have to go commando under his sweats.

Gritting her teeth against the stinging pain from the

welts and complaints from muscles tightened by cold, she pulled Mitch's T-shirt on. The dark cotton smelled of laundry soap, but because it was a different soap than hers, the sharp scent impacted her.

The shirt's hem hit well down her thigh. She knew the guy was big, but the proof of how big in comparison to her made her very aware of herself as a woman. The needs he'd brought to life out on the porch swing earlier stirred again.

"How're you doing in there?" Mitch asked through the door.

"Fine." Her answer sounded a little strangled. She had to raise her body temperature more than she had to get a grip, so she picked up the bundle of clothes and held it to her chest while she opened the bathroom door.

Mitch was right there and took her wadded-up clothes without hardly a glance at her. But he only took two steps before he stopped. He looked at her clothes, then back at her, his blue eyes sharp with concern. He promptly dropped the clothes with a wet plop on the floor and came back to her in the bathroom doorway.

Before Alison could react, he bent and caught her behind the knees with one arm and scooped her up against his chest. She instinctively made a grab for his neck with her hands and was assaulted by his heat, strength and scent as she had been that first day.

She squawked, "Mitch! What are you doing?"

"Praying you don't already have hypothermia. It's not like you're sporting a hell of a lot of insulation, woman," he grumbled without looking at her as he carried her into the kitchen toward the back door. "We need to get you warm. I'll take care of your clothes later."

Though the big towels he had over his shoulders acted as bumpers between them, the hem of the T-shirt had ridden up and her hip and thigh were pressed against his startlingly smooth, warm belly. She was also very aware of the heat of his arm against the cold, sensitive skin on the back of her knees. Not only were their faces very close, the vulnerable spot beneath his ear and the strong angle of his whisker-roughened jaw were a mere breath away from her mouth....

Mitch looked at her at that moment as if he'd heard her thoughts, his gaze on her mouth before rising to her eyes. He couldn't be a mind reader, but he was clearly aware of the intimacy of the situation, of the sensations they'd unwisely dabbled in earlier that evening.

He pushed his way through the screen door and returned his attention to where he was going. "Hang on," he warned a second before he removed his hand from her back to grab something by the door.

Alison hadn't realized how warm the house was until a blast of freezing air hit the bare skin on the backs of her thighs. She gasped. "Oh, my goodness!"

Then Mitch stepped from beneath the porch's cover to the edge of the hot tub and the pelting, near-freezing rain hit them.

And she thought she was cold before.

She exclaimed, "Coming back out here is a good thing because…?"

"Because of this." He stepped on a button that started the bubbling jets and dropped to a knee to lower her gently into the steaming tub.

The hot water took her breath away as effectively as being doused in cold water would have had she been too warm. As she panted her way through the pain until the heat started to work its magic on her, she kept busy trying to keep her T-shirt from floating upward in the riot of bubbles. Mitch opened a huge green-and-gold Colorado State University stadium umbrella and held it over them.

Through teeth clenched against the extreme sensations, Alison said, "That'll work."

Mitch set their towels on the deck behind her head, then eased into the hot tub next to her. For the first time she got a look at his bare upper body. Her heart immediately lodged in her throat. The man was beautiful, his body sculpted to perfection by hard physical labor and good health. As he moved deeper into the water, the washboard muscles in his stomach bunched beneath his smooth, tanned skin.

He turned and fit the umbrella's straight handle into a hole cut in the edge of the tub and released it. The umbrella dropped down until the bottom of the handle hit wood with a *thunk*, just far enough down so that their heads and towels were protected but high enough that they could see out across the yard and the vistas beyond. Which at the moment consisted of nothing but rain falling in sheets.

He settled himself low on the seat next to her, their shoulders touching. "I keep thinking I should add on to the porch cover for nights like this, but it's so great to sit out here in the summer and be able to look up at the millions of stars, or be kept cool by snow falling on you in the winter. And this—" he indicated the oversize umbrella "—works okay, as long as the wind isn't blowing too hard."

She nodded. "Yes, it does. Very ingenious. And it's actually kind of neat how the steam collects under here. Makes it even warmer." Cozier. More romantic. Alison closed her eyes and slid lower in the water. This wasn't about romance. It was about a nice guy trying to make sure his guest didn't bite it from hypothermia.

Mitch took one of her hands from her lap where she'd been holding the T-shirt down and started a gentle massage on her knuckles and fingers. "Yeah. Kind of our own little world under here."

Struggling to cling to the he-just-wanted-her-alive theory for her sanity's sake, Alison answered with "Mmm-hmm."

She tried to focus on the barest hint of chlorine tainting the steam and the throb of her welts, but the music of the gurgling water and soothing warmth overrode any negatives. There was nothing for her to do but accept how wonderful the moment was. She'd worry about getting Mitch to Dependable in a minute. Or an hour. Just not right now.

Mitch worked loose the muscles in one hand, then

gave the other one similar treatment. The temptation to melt beneath the surface and simply float around in the pleasure increased with each soothing rub.

While keeping hold of her hand, he gingerly slipped his other arm around her shoulders. He leaned so he could see where he placed his hand in obvious deference to her sore spots, and drew her closer against him. "Feeling better?" He raised his hand from her shoulder to stroke her hair away from her face.

The tender familiarity of the touch filled her with such yearning for a deeper connection with him, she feared she'd explode. "Much."

"That's why I installed the tub. It's easier to take the hours of working in the cold when you know you can get warmed up fast when you're done."

It seemed all Alison needed for a quick warm-up was to be nestled against a certain cowboy's side.

He cleared his throat. "You know, I really appreciate how you helped me out tonight. You didn't have to do it."

"I know. But I wanted to."

"Why?"

"Because you needed me to."

He shifted, as if he was about to get all indignant over the implication that he might not have been man enough to handle it on his own.

She rushed to add, "And because I like you and wanted to help you out."

The smile that spread across his face was crooked and heart-melting. "You like me, huh?"

The puddle that was once her heart spread in her chest. "Yeah. I like you."

He wrapped a wet curl around his finger. "Well, it seems I feel the same about you, Miss Sullivan. I haven't met a woman like you in a long time."

Not entirely sure she wanted to know, she asked, "And what sort of woman would that be?"

"The kind I admire and respect."

His unexpected compliment made her spirit soar so high she didn't know what to say. So she gave him a wide-eyed look of mock horror. "You don't admire and respect Mabel?"

He laughed. "Yes, but she doesn't make me want to do this." He lowered his mouth slowly to hers, blatantly giving her the opportunity to move away if she wanted to as he had the first time he'd kissed her.

And she wanted to even less than she had before. She curled her fingers around the hand that still held hers beneath the water. This man had the unique power to make her feel good regardless of what else was going on, regardless of what she *should* be feeling. Which was scared. She should be scared out of her mind for letting him closer than she'd ever intended, for caring far more than was wise.

But at that precise moment she once again gave herself permission to stop thinking of this as part of her all-important job. What was evolving between them felt separate from what she'd come to this ranch for.

Separate and worth it.

She'd simply have to make sure she didn't allow herself to get in too deep.

She parted her lips slightly and accepted his kiss, knowing full well what to expect this time, what power his mouth wielded.

He didn't disappoint. He captured her mouth with his and instantly set her blood on fire. She angled more toward him as he tangled his hand in her hair, holding her close. He kissed her thoroughly, deeply, until they both needed to come up for air.

Mitch released her hand and brought the other one up to cup her face, the warm water actually feeling cool against her heated skin. In the shadows beneath the umbrella she couldn't see his expression clearly.

"Man, Alison. You are so beautiful."

The thickness in his voice told her what she couldn't see. He was affected, too. There was an honesty there that she'd never heard from a man before.

Scott had expected her to look good, as if it was one of her jobs. Another one she'd never performed quite well enough. With nothing more than a simple comment and the way he looked at her, Mitch made her feel as if her appeal was a basic part of her.

The knowledge that he didn't want to feel the way he did about her made the reality so much more powerful.

In an attempt to make it easier for him, she joked, "Lucky for me you find mud and helmet hair so attractive."

He smiled in appreciation. "When they're paired with a gorgeous body, legs that never end and green eyes sparking with personality, I do." He kissed her again, savoring her lower lip before lifting his head.

Alison couldn't help grinning like an idiot. "Here I was thinking it was because I ride a mean ATV."

"That, too. That, too." He sucked in a breath and his thumb stroked where he'd just kissed her. "You have no idea how badly I want to plaster you against me right now."

The riot within her slowed, easing to a stop to give her a stunning moment of clarity. It felt right, being with this man. She wanted this with him. To hell with going it alone.

For one night.

Her throat tightened with certainty. She whispered, "What's stopping you?"

He stroked her cheek. "About a dozen welts scattered over a certain stubborn lady's arms and shoulders."

"I thought you were the creative type." She stood as best she could under the protection of the umbrella and put her hands on his shoulders. "I'm very disappointed in you, Mr. Smith." Though exposed to the air, his smooth skin felt warm, the muscles beneath hard but supple. "There aren't any welts on the insides of my thighs." She placed his legs between hers. "Or on my knees." She knelt on the seat, straddling his lap. "Or on the backs of my legs, or my bottom."

He raised his brows and reached for her waist to steady her. "When you warm up, you really warm up!"

Empowered by his earlier praise, she grinned at him.

"You have no idea." She sat down on his lap and let out an involuntary gasp. He really was affected by her.

The proof set her heart racing and turned what had started out as play into something more serious.

Could they really keep it this simple? Nothing more than a man and woman needing a momentary connection?

Didn't she deserve to feel good, to feel alive, for one night?

Mitch gripped her hips with his hands and dropped his head back with a groan of pleasure.

The sound transferred to the pit of her stomach, flooding her with heat of her own making. She flexed her fingers on his shoulders.

"Alison."

A question, or a warning? Did she know the answer? Or have it in her to use caution with him?

The answer to all her questions seemed to be a resounding yes. And to hell with caution. She wanted to experience everything she'd been denying herself.

If only for one night.

The thought popped into her head that they could have a future together if he did as the McCoys wished and moved to Dependable, joining the family and business. It was a foolish thought, she knew—a fantasy, really—but tonight seemed to be a night for fantasies.

She dipped her head and kissed him. "It's okay, Mitch. Isn't it?"

"If you're sure. I don't want to hurt you."

She could tell he didn't mean only physically. This man took care. Because of it he'd earned her trust.

She lowered her head and kissed him with meaning and purpose. He pulled her forward, moving her against him, making her burn for him.

Her head bumped against the umbrella. The wet cotton covering her breasts both chafed and caressed. His hands slid lower on her hips, then back up beneath the T-shirt he'd given her to wear. The water tempered the rough calluses on his hands, but the path he chose was surer this time than when they'd been on the porch swing.

Their time together, working as a team, seemed to have closed that last bit of distance between them. They could now be friends as well as lovers.

Such fantasies.

He moved his mouth to her jaw, her throat. "I swear I'd only meant to warm you up."

"Mmm. You did. A lot."

He grunted and kissed her pulse point, then nuzzled her ear. "But you're so great. You look so good. Make me feel so good. I can't help it." He tickled her earlobe with his tongue, finally breathing out, "All I want to do is make love to you, Alison."

She pulled in a steamy, deep, decisive breath. "Then do it, Mitch. Do it."

Chapter Ten

Mitch grabbed hold of Alison's silk-covered bottom and surged to his feet. The umbrella balanced on her head, the handle whacking against his back until it came to rest. She giggled and wrapped her long legs around his waist but didn't hang on all that tight. Clearly she trusted him not to drop her.

He hadn't really expected her to agree to making love, to want him as much as he wanted her. The fact that she had, that she apparently did, would have popped his hat right off his head had he been wearing the thing.

He stepped out of the tub and carried her toward the back door, taking half the tub's water with them. Hopefully he wouldn't trip over their boots or slip on his wet feet.

Alison pulled the umbrella from her head and dropped it on the porch to roll around its handle in a circle, then looked over her shoulder. She must intend to help by navigating.

He asked, "Front seat driver?"

She laughed. "Always willing to do my part."

Instead she managed to distract him with her tempting throat and delicate jaw line.

He'd gone from wanting Alison Sullivan, Private Investigator Extraordinaire, out of his life forever to wanting to be much more than just friends with her.

Weird night.

Actually not so weird, considering how incredible she looked stripped down to nothing but one of his T-shirts. Even without the bad-ass boots and the urban armor of her black clothes, she'd won his respect and become a woman he could connect to. A woman he could see himself partnering with. At least in this.

For tonight.

When he reached the door, Alison released her hold on his neck with one hand and pulled open the screen. He hadn't bothered to close the actual door on the way out, being too concerned with getting rid of the blue tinge to her lips to take the time. He took the time now, however, elbowing the back door closed behind him.

The little helper she was, Alison pushed on the door with her foot to get it to latch tight, then offered, "If you hold still, I might be able to turn the lock with my toes."

Chuckling, Mitch shook his head. "As entertaining as I would probably find that trick, there's no need. Hoss sees to security around here." He jerked his head toward his old dog, snoring away on his green-and-black-checked dog bed.

Alison nodded sagely, her beautiful blue-green eyes wide in mock seriousness. "I feel much safer knowing that."

"I'm glad. I wouldn't want your mind on anything other than this." He ducked his head beneath her chin and kissed the hollow above her collarbone.

"As if!" she said, laughing.

Loving the rich sound of her laughter and the way it filled him up with something mighty satisfying, he carried her out of the kitchen and down the hall, tasting her throat and neck the entire way. By the time he reached the stairs, her grip with her legs had tightened to better the contact between them and she'd threaded her fingers into his hair. Apparently he wasn't the only one thinking it was time to get serious again.

His body was already very serious about making love with Alison Sullivan. She tasted so good, even where the small amount of chlorine that he used in the hot tub had washed away the rain and salt of hard work. He took the first three steps up the stairs, but by then he'd reached her mouth with his again. She opened for him and arched against him at the same time, damn near buckling his knees with her passion.

Pausing for a moment wasn't such a bad idea, considering the mind-blowing effects of her kiss. Mitch lowered her to the dark-brown runner-cushioned stairs, soaking-wet clothes and all. He was careful to settle her atop his forearm, cradling her head in one hand while keeping his other filled with her firm, luscious bottom. Her silky panties didn't hold much water, but they did a hell of a job holding on to the heat. Or maybe it was just the fact that Alison was like liquid fire against him, setting him ablaze everywhere they touched.

The feel of her body against his had been incredible as he carried her, but when he settled on top of her, he realized he'd never wanted a woman more. He showed her as much with his kiss, doing with his tongue what he could only hint at with a grind of his hips.

She hadn't unwound her legs from around his waist, and he just about did himself in right then and there, the contact was so hot. With only her black panties and his swim trunks between them, it wouldn't take much for them to get busy on the stairs.

Tempting as it was to be a part of her as soon as possible, Mitch rejected the idea. He wanted to give her as much passion as possible more than he wanted his own. Frankly, his brain didn't have the blood supply at the moment to figure out why. At least he was lucid enough to remember his condoms were a long way away in his bedside dresser drawer.

Between kisses he said, "Must. Get. To bed."

She untangled a hand from his hair and slipped it between them, caressing him through his swim trunks. "Why?" she purred. "I think the stairs are working just fine."

Mitch grit his teeth and focused on the looped wool yarn of the runner on the stair above her bronze head to maintain the control her clever hand was trying to talk him out of. "We need protection. I have some upstairs."

Her hand froze, then moved to his side. "You're right. I can't believe I didn't think of that."

He lowered his gaze to hers and smiled to ease the worry he found there. "You didn't because I wanted you thinking of only this—" he dropped his head and licked the spot where her heart visibly throbbed in her throat "—remember?"

She lifted her chin and moaned. "Not likely to forget that, Mr. Smith."

Satisfaction surged right along with his need for her. "Good. Now, hang on again."

She didn't. "You'll hurt yourself. I can get myself to your bed on my own power."

"There you go again, doubting my abilities. You should know by now that, just like you—" he lifted her off the stairs and stood "—it makes me want to prove myself all the more." He started up the stairs, watching where he was going as best he could.

She tightened her hold on him finally. "I do not doubt your abilities." As if to prove it, she let go of his neck with one hand and stroked his hair back from his face. "I just don't want you to get hurt."

Wondering if she was tossing his own words back at him, he glanced at her. She kissed him before he could tell. He pulled away enough to murmur, "I'm a big boy and can take care of myself, Miss Sullivan."

Both physically and emotionally.

HER ATTACHMENT TO THIS MAN growing by the second, Alison hugged him tight as he carried her the rest of the way up the stairs. "You're right, you know, Mitch."

"I know. About what?"

Loving his humor, not to mention his strength as he carried her easily down the hall and into a dimly lit bedroom to the left, she nuzzled his neck. He smelled of hot tub, outdoors and man. His cologne hadn't stood a chance after a night like this. "We're alike in a lot of ways."

"Uh-uh. I know the meaning of 'go away.'"

Stung, she reared back to look at him just as he lowered her onto an antique-looking wrought-iron bed covered with a chocolate-brown chenille duvet. By the low light of a bedside lamp he'd probably left on after changing earlier she could see the teasing light in his gorgeous blue eyes.

To be sure, she asked, "But you're glad I don't know the meaning of it, right?"

He barked out a laugh. "Where have you been the last couple of hours, woman?" He followed her down enough to settle himself snugly between her legs.

Sparks flew outward from that delicious pressure point and she gasped from the intensity of the sensation.

His grin was smug and wicked. "I can't believe you had to ask."

She was seized with the need to imprint the moment on her brain so she'd have it forever. She brushed a lock of wet hair from his forehead and studied his handsome face, absorbing all the ways he made her feel the best she'd felt in her life.

His grin shifted at her seriousness. Not wanting to ruin the moment with the realities of her existence, she settled for a simpler reality and commented, "I'm going to get your bed all wet."

He rocked forward and made her gasp again. "One can hope."

She giggled but pushed at his shoulders. "No, really. This T-shirt is going to soak your comforter. I don't know about you, but wet goose down isn't one of my favorite smells."

"Now there's another way we're different." But he did lift off her enough that she could sit up. He reached for the hem of the soggy shirt. "No way am I going to pass on the chance to peel this off you."

Yet he hesitated, and for a moment she thought he was going to stop because of the welts on her arms. Instead, his gaze roamed over her chest until her already-sensitized nipples tingled and hardened more.

With a soft whistle through his teeth, he shook his head. "So much for a thick T-shirt."

Relieved and feeling more powerfully feminine than she had in a very long time, she arched subtly and inhaled deeply. "Sorry," she said on the exhalation.

"Sorry my butt." He leaned forward and kissed the tip of one breast through the shirt, sucking at the wet fabric.

Hot desire leapt through her veins. She closed her

eyes and tilted her head back. "Maybe the shirt doesn't have to come off, after all," she murmured.

Mitch released her breast and kissed his way to her throat before sitting back. "We'll turn this place into a steam room if we don't take it off. Personally, I think we're going to be steamy enough as it is."

Anticipation flooding her, she smiled and lowered her chin the same time she raised her arms. "Then let's get to it."

"Yes, ma'am." He lifted the shirt hem as far as her breasts, then stopped. "Promise you'll tell me if anything hurts, okay?"

She arched and dropped her head back again in the hopes of distracting him. "Hon, there are enough endorphins rampaging through me right now that I wouldn't notice if I'd been hit by a truck."

"Promise."

She met his gaze. The depth of concern, of caring, in his blue eyes touched her soul. "I promise, Mitch."

He kissed her sweetly and lifted the wet T-shirt up and off her. He tossed it at a plastic laundry basket set in one corner of the long room. It landed right on target with a wet *plop*. There was enough heat in his gaze this time when it traveled over her that she decided she'd never be cold again.

When he touched her, covering one fair breast with his work-scared, sun-kissed hand, she was sure. At least one corner of her heart would always be warmed by the memory of being with Mitch Smith.

Even if for only one night.

He cupped her face with his other hand. "You're so damn beautiful, Alison."

While she'd been told as much before in her life, no one had ever said it with such conviction, such emotion. Exactly what those emotions were, she wasn't sure. She could barely think with his hands on her.

He caressed his way upward from her breast to an already receding welt on her shoulder. "I'll try to be careful with you."

Not doubting it for a moment, she skimmed her hand down the muscled terrain of his chest. "Just make love to me, Mitch. Please."

His pupils flared and he kissed her hard but pulled her against him gently, plastering her to him the way he'd said he wanted to earlier. Alison wrapped her arms around him and held him just as tightly. All of the wonderful sensations of before paled in comparison to the feel of his skin against hers.

The thudding of his heart against her breasts melted every barrier she might have managed to leave up between them.

Just as the need to earn his trust had seized her earlier, she now was overcome by the compulsion to somehow make him feel as good as he made her feel. To that end, she moved her hand down to the waistband of his swimsuit, slipping her fingers beneath the elastic, then sliding forward to his belly. When she moved back to allow room for her arm, he pulled away.

"You'll press on those welts if you do that."

She did her darnedest to match his earlier naughty grin. "I was aiming to press on something else."

"Not this go-around, darlin'." He moved back, forcing her to release him completely.

Before she could protest, he got off the bed and pulled the comforter and sheet back, encouraging her to lift up so he could get it out from underneath her. The cream-colored sheet was cold.

He gestured toward the pillow. "I want you to lie back and take it easy. I'll do everything."

Despite the fact that she was as bare-chested as he was, she planted her hands on her panty-clad hips. "Now, what about me makes you think I'd enjoy that?"

"Suffer through it for my sake, please. I won't enjoy myself if I'm worrying about you hurting yourself."

He shucked his swim trunks and her argument died in her throat.

Golden. Everything about the man was beautifully formed, hard and *golden.* "You normally don't wear a swimsuit, do you?"

He spared a glance downward and laughed. "Not when I'm by myself. Don't get a lot of drop-in visitors." He climbed onto the bed next to her and covered them up, encouraging her to lie back on one of the two plush pillows.

"Except me." She instantly regretted the reminder of why she was here, of how she'd dropped into his life and disrupted everything.

Mitch's mind appeared firmly entrenched elsewhere as he traced a path between her breasts, down her belly, to the edge of her panties. "Would you have been shocked if I'd been in the buff when you pulled up?" He pushed her panties downward, urging them off.

She reached down to help. "More likely impressed."

He chuckled and allowed her to shimmy out of her undies. "Really?"

"Very," she vowed.

He moved her arm out of his way and rolled partway onto her. "Okay, now you're patronizing me."

His weight was heavenly and his consideration heart-melting. "Not for a second, Mr. Smith."

They were both smiling when he kissed her, but it didn't take long for the playfulness to give way to earnest, passionate lovemaking. And despite having sworn on all she considered sacred never to be dependent on a man again, Alison found herself truly, deeply enjoying allowing Mitch to call the shots.

She actually found being dependent on him incredibly satisfying. It didn't hurt that he was a generous lover.

He kissed and touched every inch of her, slipping under the covers to keep her from getting chilled.

She ended up *hot*.

When he finally donned the protection he'd dug out of a bedside drawer and became one with her, filling her in a way she'd never experienced before, it dawned on her that she was in serious, *serious* trouble.

And when he brought her to a climax that shattered

her from the inside out, she had to admit to herself that she had gone and fallen in love with one Mitchell Davis Smith of Whiskey Ridge, Colorado. A Lost Millionaire determined to stay lost.

What had she done?

Chapter Eleven

A creature of habit, Mitch woke before dawn. Since it was June, that meant *way* early. His room was dark, the bedside light having been turned off at some point in the night. After he'd dug the third foil packet out of the drawer, if he remembered correctly. Though a hint of light did make it up from downstairs, where nothing had been turned off.

Because they'd both been too turned on.

Alison was still nestled tight against him. He couldn't manage to bring himself to feel sorry about what had happened between them. He probably should, but he didn't.

Whether Alison had wanted to slip out after he'd finally succumbed and fallen into an exhausted sleep, he didn't know. He hadn't given her the chance. After they'd made love the last time, he'd spooned her up tight against him with his arm around her waist and hadn't let go.

She was so warm and pliant against him, her breathing soft and even, her hair like twirled silk against his face. Contentment made his limbs heavy. He didn't think he'd ever felt this comfortable cuddled up to a woman in his life. Something about the way she fit against him, maybe. Or the way he could so easily imagine her fitting into his life for good.

Now, there was a thought he would have bet against having a mere twenty-four hours ago. Then he'd simply wanted her and the mess she'd brought with her gone. But in the time since she'd stepped up on his porch to have dinner with him, the woman had completely changed his perception of her.

He nuzzled her copper hair, breathing in the faint scent of rain with a hint of hot tub. She was caring and giving, and her integrity was bolstered by a mighty dose of stubbornness he admired.

Absolutely nothing like Krissi Torella.

And unlike with Krissi, this morning he didn't have the urge to get Alison up and out of there before his men arrived for work. With Krissi, he'd told her—and himself—he was hurrying her home out of respect for her, for her reputation. In hindsight he realized he'd been doing it to keep the speculation and ribbing to a minimum.

Maybe he'd known somewhere deep in his gut that Krissi hadn't been the woman for him, that she wasn't the helpmate he wanted. She sure as hell wouldn't have hopped on an ATV to help him save a bunch of calves, even when his future might depend on them.

The thought of his uncertain future dampened his

mood big time. There were some decisions to be made, and now something new to consider.

If he sold all of the calves instead of using them to strengthen his own herd, he'd have more than enough money to make payments on two mortgages for some time.

Maybe enough to also help a pretty P.I. with her financial woes so she could stick around a little while longer. Long enough for them to find out if they were really as well matched as they seemed.

Everything in him stilled at the prospect.

As if sensing the change in him, Alison stirred, her hips shifting and rubbing against him, her face burrowing deeper into the pillow. Then she stiffened.

She was probably still too sleepy to realize where she was. He hated that. Not wanting her to be afraid for a second, he rushed to reassure her. "It's okay, sweetheart," he murmured, his voice rougher than normal from shouting over the storm and the roar of the ATVs. "You're here with me, in my bedroom."

Where you belong.

Mitch blinked, startled by the wayward thought.

Alison groaned and put a hand over her face.

It wasn't exactly the reaction he'd been expecting. Or hoping for, to be honest. It stung a bit.

"I can't believe I actually fell asleep here." She relaxed her body and rubbed her bare feet along his as she straightened her legs. "What time is it, do you know?"

He lifted his head high enough to see the glowing

numbers on his nightstand digital clock. "It's not quite five yet."

She stiffened again. "It'll be light soon."

He splayed his hand over her smooth, flat belly, desire stirring, also. "This time of year, yep." He pressed himself against her perfect backside. "But that doesn't mean the night has to be over."

She pushed herself up on an elbow and looked at the window on the wall opposite the bed. He hadn't closed the curtains, which matched the comforter cover, and a faint, predawn glow tinted the eastern horizon. "But won't your crew be arriving then?"

"No doubt. I'm sure they spent the night worrying about whether I was able to get those calves undercover before that hail hit." He ran his hand over the curve of her hip, remembering what a perfect handhold it had been. Now he *really* didn't want to get out of bed.

"I'd better get moving." She sat up the rest of the way and swung her legs to the side of the mattress, slipping out from under his hand. Her wild curls spilled in a glorious mess down her slender, pale back and drew his interest to the slight dimples above her bottom that practically demanded to be kissed.

He reached for her. The last thing any sane man would want to see was a woman like Alison bailing out of his bed. "No need." He snagged her around the waist and gently hauled her back toward him.

"'Fraid so. I've already compromised my job enough

as it is. I shouldn't be seen here this early. They'll know I spent the night."

Damn integrity. He grinned and went looking for her neck under all that wonderful hair. "So?"

She pulled away from him. "*So?* What do you mean, *so?* I thought you were listening last night at dinner, Mitch. I need this job."

He made a decision right then and there. "Maybe not."

"If what I did were to somehow get back to the Mc-Coys—what?" She shifted a knee onto the bed so she could turn completely toward him. "What do you mean, *maybe not?*"

He traced a circle on her hip. "How about I loan you the money you need to get solvent again? That is, as much as I can while still repaying the McCoys and making my loan payment on the ranch."

Her jaw dropped.

He lifted up enough to take advantage of her open mouth. She kissed him back, but her focus was clearly elsewhere. He pulled back, happier than he'd been in a long time. A good sign.

Her mouth was still hanging open.

He grinned. Without a doubt, helping her was the right thing to do. Especially if it kept her around awhile longer. He wasn't ready for Alison Sullivan to walk out of his life yet. What that would mean in the future, he wasn't sure.

He noticed a perfectly formed spiral of coppery hair caught on the ridge of her collarbone.

He'd worry about the future later.

She finally spoke. "You have got to be joking."

He forced himself to ignore her hair and the creamy skin on her throat and tempting breasts, and looked her in the eye. "I'm one hundred percent serious. The cash I have on hand isn't near enough to pay back the McCoys with, so I'd have to wait until an additional loan goes through to get clear of them, anyhow. I might as well use my cash now to help you out then replace it with money from selling most of those prime calves."

It would also get her out from under the possibly negative control of the McCoys, but he knew she'd definitely argue that point so he didn't make it.

Her mouth dropped open again, but this time she closed it with a snap and climbed out of bed. Though it was still pretty dark in the room, he swore she looked as if she was going to be sick. Her shoulders curved forward and her movements were jerky.

Mitch's heart stuttered in his chest, and dread spread through him like ice on a window. He sat up. "Alison?"

She reached under the covers and searched around until she found her black panties.

His heart started to pound the way it did when he bucked hundred-pound hay bales. "Alison."

She put her underwear on with abrupt movements. "That's not why I slept with you, Mitch." The quaver in her voice confirmed she was upset.

A chill that made the icy wind of the night before seem like a balmy breeze slipped beneath his skin. "Of course not! I never suggested you did. How could I when the thought never entered my head?"

Her arms crossed over her breasts, she rounded the bed, muttering, "I swore I'd make it on my own and I will." She headed for the white plastic hamper as if she intended to put back on the T-shirt she'd worn into the hot tub. Which would still be wet.

The fact that she not only didn't want his help, but wanted to get away from him that badly hit him like a bull's kick to the chest. He bolted out of bed and charged to his dresser. "I have another pair of sweats, Alison." He pulled out a dark blue set that was splattered with paint but infinitely better than a wet T-shirt.

"That's okay. I'll just go down and get my own clothes to wear back to the motel." She grabbed a bath towel from the hamper and wrapped it around her.

An unexpected dose of panic flooded him. He told himself it was from the thought of her leaving so upset. Not simply the fact that she was leaving.

No, dammit, it *was* because she was leaving. He didn't want her to.

Mitch tossed the sweats onto the bed then yanked out a pair of jeans from the dresser and put them on as fast as he could, only buttoning a couple of buttons. Careful where he touched her, he caught her in the bedroom doorway, the towel gripped with both fists.

He hissed again at the round, golf-ball-size bruises already forming here and there on her shoulders and arms. She'd gone through so much to help him, he didn't want her to suffer anymore on his account.

She wouldn't look at him, so he caught her under the chin with his knuckle and turned her face to his. The light from downstairs was strong enough to glisten off the tears filling her beautiful eyes.

Her unhappiness seared him like a branding iron to the heart. "Please, Alison, don't cry. I swear I don't think you slept with me for money, or to get your way, or anything like that." His throat tight, he stroked her hair back away from her face. "I was kinda hoping what happened last night happened because you...have feelings for me?"

She closed her eyes and, after a moment, nodded so slightly he would have missed it if he hadn't been holding her chin.

He was ridiculously relieved, considering how reluctant she'd been to admit to her feelings for him. "Okay, then." He released her chin. "Now, please put on the sweats, sweetheart. Your clothes never made it to the washer or dryer, remember? They're probably still wet considering they were left in a pile on the floor."

Her shoulders slumped more. "So much for a quick getaway."

He hated seeing her looking so defeated, but the hint of her humor relieved him mightily. "Sorry. I guess you're stuck here with me for a little longer."

She straightened, looking him in the eye. "Not your fault. I distracted you when you had my clothes."

He ran a knuckle down her soft cheek. "That you did,

darlin'. That you did." He held out a hand to urge her to precede him back into the bedroom.

She retrieved the sweats from the bed and pulled them on beneath the towel, then turned her back to him before removing the towel and putting on the too-big sweatshirt. Her modesty cut him after the intimacy they'd shared in the night. How had he managed to screw up so badly, so fast?

Finally, she faced him, her expression similar to the one she'd worn when she'd first approached him at the front corral what seemed like ages ago.

The P.I. with a job to do was back.

Dammit, anyway. While he admired her commitment to her job, it was the woman he wanted to spend time with.

Before he could tell her to forget he ever opened his stupid mouth, her gazed dipped down his chest to the half-buttoned fly of his jeans. She closed her eyes and inhaled deeply, as if bracing herself against temptation and need.

Maybe all wasn't lost. If sex was what she wanted from him right now, fine.

At least he'd have more time with her.

ALISON MENTALLY COUNTED to ten before she dared to open her eyes and look again at the gorgeous, wonderful man in front of her. She couldn't allow herself to slip back into the fantasy she'd indulged in with him. His offer to help her financially had been the dose of reality she'd needed to snap her out of the dream world she'd spent the night in.

Old hurts were rubbed raw again. Why couldn't anyone believe she had it in her to solve her own problems?

Probably because she never had.

She'd sat around on her parents' farm waiting for someone to save her from a life she hadn't wanted. When she'd met Scott at her friend Kelly's wedding, he'd seemed like a knight in a red Miata come to whisk her away from the tedium. Which he had, until someone else caught his eye.

She forced the self-pity aside and straightened her shoulders to look at Mitch. So what if no one respected her, as long as she could respect herself. She had no choice but to reject Mitch's offer. She'd vowed to make it on her own, and that was exactly what she was going to do.

But the sight of him bed-mussed with his jeans only half buttoned... She sighed and closed her eyes again. The intense concern and respectfulness on his handsome face made the backs of her eyes burn.

Why did he have to be the perfect man? Why did he have to be so honorable, trustworthy, funny and a great cook? Her gaze strayed across the sculpted muscles of his chest, shoulders and arms. Why did he have to be so perfect for her?

She met his blue eyes, turbulent with worry, and her heart succumbed. Why was he so easy to love?

"Alison, talk to me. What just happened here?"

The bite of frustration and an aching heart made her laugh harshly. "A nasty thing I'm forced to claim as my reality, Mitch."

"What does that mean?"

"It means I stepped into an amazing fantasy the second you put me in that tub. Heck, the second you looked at me. But your little offer of charity snapped me out of it, reminded me what I'm here for."

He pulled his chin back. "I am not offering you *charity,* Alison."

"Then what exactly are you offering me?"

"The help that will allow us to have a chance to see where things could go between us. How about that?"

Alison's world tilted and she had to grab on to the bed's wrought-iron footboard to keep from losing her balance. She couldn't believe he'd actually put to words what her heart had been begging for all night. The one thing that couldn't be.

She turned and sat down on the edge of the bed. "There's only one problem with that, Mitch."

He hooked his thumbs in the belt loops of his jeans and shifted his weight to one leg. "Which is?"

The words threatened to choke her, but she forced them out. "I'm not the woman for you." He wanted someone to help him achieve his goals. She needed to prove she could achieve her own, that she could go it alone.

His laugh was disbelieving. "I think the third time last night disproved that."

"I'm not talking about our physical attraction."

He gave her a level look. "Neither am I."

Her heart tripped, then took off at a run as irrational hope roared through her. But an honest-to-goodness relationship with Mitch couldn't be. She shook her head against the mists of fantasy threatening to engulf her again. "No. It can't work. You said yourself that you want a helpmate. I've already tried being a man's partner in life and it cost me dearly."

He raised his hands. "Hey, whoa. Hold it right there." He moved to stand directly in front of her, his muscle-marred flat stomach rising and falling quickly. "First off, I'm *nothing* like your ex."

She dropped her head into her hands. "Trust me, I'm more than aware of that. I didn't mean to imply it."

"Then what did you mean?"

"I made a promise to myself. A vow, really."

"To do what? Spend the rest of your days alone? To martyr yourself?"

Horror flashed through her, but she closed her mind to the image he'd created. She had to face one worry at a time. She couldn't think that far ahead.

She dropped her hands into her lap, absently noting the red spots on her palm that would have been blisters if Mitch hadn't given her gloves to wear while driving his ATV. The grip her newfound love for him had on her heart tightened to a nearly unbearable squeeze. He'd been so good to her, he deserved an explanation.

Despite the regret thick in her throat, she said, "To prove that I can make it on my own."

The weight of his hand settled on her hair, then moved downward as he gently stroked her head. She was swamped by the need to wrap her arms around his hips and press her face tight to his bare belly. He would be so easy to give herself up to, to depend upon for everything.

But how could she respect herself afterward?

Damn.

She lurched off the bed and away from him. She'd been so wrong to think she was strong enough to allow herself this time with him. At this rate she'd end up proving Scott and her father right about not being able to make it on her own before the day was out.

The awful truth was, now that Mitch had made his offer, she couldn't have anything to do with him and expect to hang on to a modicum of her self-respect. He might even come to doubt her reasons for being with him.

There was only one course of action left for her.

"Alison, sweetheart, please. Accepting help from me—in the form of a *loan*—doesn't equal not making it on your own."

"It's not like you're some bank, Mitch. No matter how you cut it, it's not the same."

He ran his hands through his hair where her fingers had been tangled only hours before. The stunning, sharp pain of loss threatened to double her over. She stiffened her spine against the weakness.

"It might not be the same, but refusing my help when you need it so much is downright foolish. I just don't get how an obviously smart woman like you can be so…so…"

Though she knew with the certainty of a sure heart that Mitch wouldn't purposefully hurt her as Scott had, the fact that Mitch had stumbled down a similar path awoke the outrage she'd need to get through this. She arched a brow at him and supplied, "Stupid?"

"Foolish!"

"So it's foolish of me to want to be independent? To want to prove I have in me what it takes to make it without any help? Would you accuse your neighbor of the same thing? Or Carl?"

"Maybe."

"But only after you'd slept with them, right?"

He threw his hands up in exasperation. "Please."

"Look, Mitch, I think we have no choice but to face the fact that we don't belong together."

"How can you be so sure? From what I've seen so far, I think we make one hell of a team. Frankly, I'd like the chance to find out if it could last."

Her heart slammed against her ribs as if it were trying to get to him, to the promise of a blissful future in his arms. She refused to be that weak, to take such an easy road.

Hating that she'd put herself in this situation in the first place, irrationally hating Mitch for being so amazing, she lashed out. "You want a foreman, not a wife."

He took a step back, as if she'd physically pushed him away. "Why are you doing this?"

Because she had to push him away. "I have to end this now. I have to accept the inevitable. I can't be with you and preserve my self-respect."

He frowned fiercely, looking as if he was about to

argue, so she stopped him before he could speak. "Look, I've got to go. I have things to do." Phone calls to make. Her stomach made a sickening roll.

She hurried past him, hoping he wouldn't stop her while the weak part of her wished he would.

He didn't.

She gritted her teeth and made herself leave the bedroom and go down the stairs. The nubby texture of the carpet runner on her bare feet reminded her of what it'd felt like beneath her hips and back where the wet T-shirt had ridden up. Other memories of what had happened on those stairs mere hours ago filled her eyes with tears. She was afraid to blink for fear they'd go spilling down her face. Mitch didn't deserve to be left with the guilt of having made her cry on top of everything else.

She snagged her big black purse from beneath the table at the bottom of the stairs, then hurried toward the other end of the hall where her clothes still lay in a pile near the doorway to the kitchen. She snatched them up and headed across the cold linoleum to her boots. The temptation to simply grab them, also, and run out to her rental truck in her bare feet was strong, but since this entire exit was suppose to be about preserving her dignity, she resisted the urge.

She sat down in the same chair she'd used to strip her boots off and dumped her damp, dirty clothes on the floor again so she could put her boots back on.

Hoss slowly pushed to his feet and ambled over to her from his bed, the tags on his brown leather collar jingling and his bottom wagging. If his unconditional affection wasn't enough to make her cry, she didn't know what was. She blinked rapidly and tried to ignore the old dog.

"So that's it?" Mitch asked from the doorway, startling her. She hadn't heard him come down. Halfway hadn't expected him to. Because he'd been right; they were a lot alike in many ways. If the situation had been reversed, her stubborn pride probably would have kept her upstairs, fuming. But Mitch was a better person than she.

Her heart tore in two because this had to be it. She forced her foot into one boot, then shoved the white-paint-stained sweatpant leg to her knee so she could zip the boot closed. Yeah, this was going to be a cute outfit to storm off in. So much for dignity.

Everything was going wrong. So, so wrong.

She waited until she had a foot in the other boot before she answered. "Yes, that's it."

"What if I don't want it to be?"

"Then come back to Dependable with me today," she blurted. If only finishing the job she'd been sent to do was her motivation for wanting to keep him in her life.

His stare didn't waver, but her heart latched on to the fact she could see his throat working. "You know I can't do that, Alison."

"You mean *won't*."

"Just like you won't stay here."

He'd hit the post square. She picked up her things and

stood, leaving her heart in their place. It took every ounce of strength she had in her, but she looked him in the eye. "That's right."

Frustration rolled off him in waves. "Are you afraid of the McCoys, Alison? For any reason?"

"Of course not." They'd given her a reason to hope.

"Really?"

"Yes. Really."

A muscled ticked in his jaw. He was such a protector. If fear of the powerful McCoys had been her motivator, she knew he would have championed her. The certainty was almost enough to make her say to hell with her vow and jump into his arms.

Almost.

"I'm sorry, Mitch."

"So am I, Alison."

Not knowing what else to say, she opted for the automatic "It was nice meeting you."

He let out a disbelieving laugh and ran a hand over his face. "You gotta be kidding me, Alison. You can't go like this—"

"I have to." She moved to the back door. Hoss nudged her, ready to join in on whatever it was she might be doing. She gave his silky head a long, heartfelt stroke, then took hold of the door handle.

"What are you going to tell the McCoys?"

She opened the back door and cold air hit her like a slap. A much-needed one. Drawing in a lungful of the bracing predawn air, she answered, "The truth. They hired the wrong person for the job. Have a good life, Mitch Smith. I'll mail you the sweats back."

She didn't give him a chance to say anything before slipping out the door and closing it behind her as quickly as she could. Which was fortunately faster than the sob that erupted from her aching, hollow chest. She put a hand over her mouth and moved away from the door.

Stubbornness sucked a lot worse than vanity.

The part of her still attached to her heart listened for the sound of the door opening behind her as she walked around the porch to the front of the house, but all she heard were the sounds of the new day waking. From the pasture behind the house a horse nickered. A cricket chirped in cadence with the sharp sound of her boot heels on wood.

Of course he wasn't going to come after her. She'd made herself painfully clear. And no matter how much she might yearn to, she wasn't going to go back in.

She shifted the bundle of clothes in her arms so she could dig in her purse for the key to the truck. She'd found it by the time she reached the truck, unmelted hail collected at the base of the windshield. Enough light glowed on the eastern horizon to allow her to see to unlock the driver's door and let herself in. She tossed her clothes onto the seat and climbed in.

Still no Mitch.

She glanced at the house as she closed the driver's door behind her. The kitchen light clicked off. Well, he deserved to go back to bed. Just like she deserved a kick in the head. Mitch had been right. She *was* foolish. But not for wanting to hold tight to some vow.

She was a fool for letting herself fall so hard and so fast for a man who should have been nothing more than part of a job.

A job she'd failed to do.

Numbness that had nothing to do with the biting temperature seeped through her. She reached for her purse and found her cell phone. Thanks to the time difference, it wouldn't be too early to get this over with. She selected the private number the patriarch of the McCoy dynasty had given to her to program into her phone.

He picked up before the second ring. "Joseph McCoy speaking."

She could just see him seated behind his huge mahogany desk in his den, not a steel-gray hair out of place, those bright McCoy-blue eyes sharp. The man had grieved hard and publicly for his son, Marcus, but then, as far as she could tell, he'd shifted that emotional energy to finding the grandsons he hadn't known he had. Or had he? Had he simply not known where to find them?

She brushed the pointless speculation aside. The McCoys were no longer her concern. "This is Alison Sullivan, Mr. McCoy." Heaven help her, she sounded the same as when her first horse had fallen into an irrigation ditch and had to be put down.

"Miss Sullivan! I've been wondering when I'd hear from you. Are you on your way back with my grandson?"

The hope and expectation in his gravelly voice sent

her chin to her chest and a pair of tears rolling down her cheeks. She gripped the truck's steering wheel with her free hand. "No, sir. I'm afraid not. That's why I'm calling."

There was silence on the other end, then, "Go on."

"Mitch Smith of Whiskey Ridge, Colorado, is indeed your grandson, sir, but I've failed to persuade him to come to Dependable with me." She looked at the dark house. "Ever. And I think you should know he stubbornly plans to repay the money Marcus paid his mother."

"Does he, now?" Joseph didn't sound too concerned. Amused, actually.

Alison grimaced and released the steering wheel only long enough to swipe at her wet cheeks, getting a hold of herself. She must not be making herself clear. "I failed to complete the job you hired me for, Mr. McCoy. Your financial obligation toward me is null."

He surprised the heck out of her by chuckling. "Don't you worry, Miss Sullivan. I'll find a way to get that boy to Dependable in time for my seventy-fifth birthday party. And you'll be compensated for your time."

She shifted her grip from the steering wheel to her forehead. Compensation for her time was more than she deserved, so she'd have no choice but to decline. And only the bonus she would have received for bringing Mitch to Dependable herself would have saved her from bankruptcy.

"Miss Sullivan?"

She straightened at his caring tone. "Yes, sir?"

"Come on home, girl. Come on home."

The tears broke free again and tumbled down her cheeks in a steady stream. Her own father had said the same thing to her when she'd told him of Scott's desertion. She'd been too stubborn and proud to heed the call then, but Joseph's words were like a Siren's song to her now. She shifted the phone to her other hand and started the truck. "I will, sir. Thank you."

Though she didn't have much to go home to, it was better than looking back.

Chapter Twelve

"You got a warrant out on you or something?"

Mitch jerked his gaze from his truck's rearview mirror to Carl in the passenger's seat. "What?"

Carl took the toothpick he'd been chewing on out of his mouth located somewhere beneath his thick black mustache and pointed at the rearview mirror. "You've been checking your tail since we left the Circle S like you're afraid Johnny Law's gonna sneak up on you."

Not the police, a bad-ass private investigator. And he wasn't afraid; he was ridiculously hopeful. Every stinking time he left the ranch a part of him always held out hope that he'd see a white rented pickup truck roaring up to dog him all the way into Whiskey Ridge.

Not having realized that what he'd been doing was noticeable, Mitch tried to cover his embarrassment with a one-shoulder shrug. "Just making sure nothing's blowing out of the bed."

Carl took a little-too-casual look-see over his shoulder. "Considering we hosed it out right before we left, I think you're safe."

Mitch shifted in his seat, silently cussing himself for the lame excuse. He could feel Carl's regard, but he stubbornly refused to come clean about what had him truly miserable now.

"If I were you—which I'm not, mind you—I'd probably be watching my back in case a certain redhead decided to darken my bumper again. She didn't exactly seem the type to just up and quit," Carl mused, and returned the toothpick to his mouth.

"Well, turns out she was," Mitch snapped, then instantly regretted it. He twisted his tight grip on the steering wheel. He couldn't seem to get a handle on his anger or anything else since Alison Sullivan marched her stiletto-heel boots out of his life six days ago.

"Now that's a shame."

Mitch quickly glanced at Carl and found him staring straight ahead, working the toothpick slowly up and down in his mouth. Mitch purposefully returned his attention to the road. "I thought you didn't like redheads."

"You clearly do. And that one definitely could make any man reconsider his previous inclinations. All that fire and backbone. Plus any woman willing to drive cattle is worth a month of lazy Sundays."

Mitch shot Carl a look again. Mitch hadn't said a word about Alison helping him herd the calves undercover, and since none of his men had asked, he'd assumed they thought he'd managed it himself.

The toothpick shifted to the other side of Carl's mustache. "Wouldn't have thought a prissy-looking thing like her would know how to treat an ATV as well as she did. After those sisters of yours take the four-wheelers out for a spin, I always have to fix the clutches."

The ATV. Mitch should have known Carl would notice they'd both been used during the storm.

Carl finally looked at him again. "Hope she was riding the black one."

The one without all the new dents. "No. She wasn't."

"She get banged up? That why she took off?" The concern in Carl's dark eyes was genuine. Mitch had worked too closely with the man for too long to doubt it.

"Yes, she got pretty banged up. She wouldn't come out of the hail until the last calf was safe. And no, that's not why she went back home."

"Judging from the way you've been acting like a bull with a horn caught in the chute since then, you should have stopped her."

The frustration and hurt he'd been wrestling with from the moment things had gone south with Alison regained its grip on his chest. "I had to let her go."

"Had to, hmm?"

"Yes. I didn't have a choice."

"Now, see, the beauty of being a cowboy is always having a choice."

Mitch snorted. "Spoken like a man with a truly agreeable wife."

Carl laughed. "There's no such thing, son."

Worried that he'd never find out for himself if he couldn't get his heart to listen to his brain, Mitch fell silent as they reached Whiskey Ridge and the point where the highway became Main Street. He adjusted his speed accordingly.

As Mitch steered his truck into an angled parking spot in front of the feed store, one storefront down from Harvey's hardware store and across the street from the bank, Carl said, "You could always go after her, you know."

"Why in Sam Hill would you think I'd want to?"

"Because it's obvious there are some things that need to be resolved between you two."

"It's obvious, huh?"

"Richie passed her in that rental truck as he turned off the highway the morning after the storm. And even if he hadn't, we would have all noticed your shorts are in a twist about something above and beyond what she came here for."

Mitch slammed the gearshift into Park and propped his wrists on the top of the steering wheel. "So is this why you wanted to come to town with me? To try to untwist my shorts?"

"Won't catch me going there. But I did think you might need a sympathetic ear."

"That's what horses are for, Carl."

The mustache twitched, but Carl was a decent poker player. "True. True. But a horse isn't going to tell you to go after a good thing."

"No, but a stubborn mule might." When Mitch's glare was met with an unrepentant stare, he blew out a breath and conceded. "She may be a good thing, but she's not the woman I need."

"You can always buy her new boots."

Mitch chuckled and shook his head at Carl's ability to keep life simple. "Trust me, her fashion sense—or rather, nonsense—is the least of our problems." He picked at the dirt beneath his nails left from this morning's work of cutting the cattle he knew would sell the fastest from the rest of the herd. "She made it abundantly clear she wants an independent life."

"An independent life?"

"She's divorced." Mitch looked at Carl to deliver the fact about Alison that had caused her so much pain. "Her ex-husband did a number on her, taking off with his receptionist while leaving her with his debt."

"So why would that keep her from getting involved with you?"

"I offered to pay off the debt."

The brim of Carl's hat went up with his eyebrows "While paying back the people who sent her?"

Mitch ran a hand over his face and unbuckled his seat belt. "I wasn't exactly thinking clearly."

"Ah. So it was *after* she'd spent the night. And here I thought you were a smart man. Money should never be discussed anywhere near the bedroom."

That earned Carl another glare before Mitch opened the truck door and climbed out. He slammed the door shut and headed for the feed store's entrance. Carl followed at his own pace.

"Mitch!"

Mitch stopped on the threshold and both he and Carl turned to look across the street where the call had come from. Donald Lichton was standing in the doorway of his bank, waving to get their attention.

Mitch gave an acknowledging wave. "Yeah, Donald?" he yelled back across the street.

The banker held up a letter-size piece of paper. "There's something I need to talk to you about. Do you have a moment?"

Dread, thick and heavy, spread through Mitch. The time for double-debt was near. "Sure, Donald." To Carl he said, "Do you mind grabbing a couple of sacks of grain for me?"

Carl tipped his sweat-stained black cowboy hat, understanding plain in his eyes. "No problem."

Mitch took a deep breath and headed back past his truck and hustled across the street before a semi-truck traveling through town, probably bound for Fort Collins, drew near.

Donald opened the glass door to the bank and held it with his free hand while Mitch stepped up onto the sidewalk. "I was just calling you when Krissi spotted your truck across the way."

"Good thing she's so observant," Mitch commented dryly as he walked by Donald and through the door.

"Better known as nosy," Donald murmured as he followed.

A smile tugged at Mitch's mouth despite his trepidation. Krissi was standing at her teller's station, counting money in her till but mostly watching them. He pulled on the brim of his hat. "Krissi."

"Hey, Mitch." Her greeting didn't exude the same sexuality as usual. She must have divined from his previous visit that he was about to be far less well off than he had been.

Fine by him. His past experiences with the pretty blonde aside, he feared a certain redhead had spoiled him for good.

Donald hurried ahead of him. "Let's go in my office."

Mitch followed him around the teller's counter to the small bank's lone enclosed office. He'd rather be following a dentist in to have all his teeth pulled sans novocaine. But he'd rather owe a couple of banks than the McCoys.

Donald gestured to one of the chairs set before his desk. "Please, have a seat."

Mitch pulled his hat from his head and sat down as Donald rounded the desk and settled into his large black-leather desk chair. Mitch set his jaw against the sick feeling engulfing him. This had to be done. No way was he going to live his life under someone's thumb.

He hung his hat on the arm of his chair. "Do you need me to sign something?"

"No. But there is something you need to know." Donald gripped between both hands the paper he'd been carrying. On closer inspection, he looked about as sick as Mitch felt.

Mitch leaned forward. "What is it?"

"I received this fax this morning. It's notification that your principal mortgage, not the additional one we've been trying to secure, has been bought from the company I'd sold it to."

"Okay…" Mitch said, wondering at Donald's behavior. Loans were bought and sold all the time by lenders and other financial institutions. He always made his payments on time, so his mortgage was a solid investment.

Donald heaved a sigh. "And the new owner is calling the note in."

"What?"

"I don't understand it, either. There's no explanation, and I've yet to receive a response from the inquiry I made the second this came through. I can't tell from this if the new owner of the loan is acting within his rights." Donald held the piece of paper out to Mitch. "I'll have to investigate further, since from the looks of it, a single person rather than a financial institution bought the loan and is demanding payment of the balance."

Donald reconsidered and shook his head. "It has to be the name of the company, though I sure don't recognize it." He tapped on the top of the page as Mitch took it.

Mitch read the name and his blood turned to ice. "No, it's a single person who bought my loan, not a financial institution."

Donald pulled in his chin. "You're kidding."

Mitch shook his head, glancing over the rest of the information contained in the fax. "I wish I was. Lord, how I wish I was. Joseph McCoy is the billionaire founder of McCoy Enterprises. Which is a general retailer. Though I wouldn't be surprised if they had their own bank, or credit union or something."

Donald frowned, the creases traveling all the way up to his balding head. "*That* Joseph McCoy? *The Don't trust it if it's not from the real McCoy* Joseph McCoy?"

Mitch ran his fingers through his hair, his mind spinning. "Yes."

"I was just in a McCoys store when I was in Denver. Broke my shoelaces right before a meeting and had to get some new ones. I also picked up a new music CD and some snacks for the drive home. Those are nice stores," Donald mused.

Holding the fax with both hands, Mitch leaned forward and rested his elbows on his knees. Joseph McCoy had bought his loan and was calling it. Whether he had the right to or not, he could probably make it happen. It would ruin Mitch. And here he'd thought he'd felt sick before.

"Why would he do this?" Donald's growing bewilderment matched the certainty swelling in Mitch's gut.

To get Mitch to give up his life here and join the McCoys in Dependable, that's why.

But how had McCoy recognized his one and only weakness so succinctly?

Alison.

She knew exactly where his soft spot was, exactly how important that loan was to him. She must have gone straight to McCoy and given up what she knew to him. How much cash had that tidbit earned her?

Not only had she run out on him, she'd sold him out. Betrayed him. The knowledge cut deeper than any of the lies he'd been told thus far in his life. A surprising and telling fact.

"Mitch?"

He glanced up from the fax he'd unwittingly crumbled between his hands to find Donald watching him worriedly. "Sorry." Donald's questions sinking in, Mitch sat back. "Ah…it's complicated."

Though actually, when he thought about it, the whole mess was quite simple. His biological father must have had an attack of conscience and decided to do right by his bastard son—make that sons, according to Alison—by putting them in his will. Now his father's family was doing everything in their power, which was certainly limitless thanks to all their money, to execute said will.

But he was now more certain than ever that he'd be damned if he'd let a bunch of strangers have that kind of power over him. He'd have to sell all his cattle and everything else that wasn't nailed down, but he'd call Joseph McCoy's bluff.

And he'd do it to his face. Some snakes needed to be looked in the eye before using your heel on them.

"Donald, I have to take a trip, but while I'm gone, could you do me a huge favor and see if you can scare up a buyer for my entire herd as well as my equipment? This last batch of calves I specially bred are really something and should generate a lot of interest."

Donald somehow managed to look more shocked than before. "Your *entire* herd? Mitch, you can't—"

Mitch grabbed his hat and pushed to his feet. "I don't have any choice, Donald. I'm also going to need a promissory note to cover that loan. If you can figure out a way to do that based on the value of what I have to sell, I'd truly appreciate it."

"But not your breeder stock—"

"I refuse to let Joseph McCoy take control of my land, Donald." The conclusion felt as right as the hat Mitch settled on his head.

A true friend, Donald stood and opened his mouth to continue to protest.

Mitch stopped him with a conclusive, "Or me."

He turned and strode from Donald's office, knowing in his gut that Alison Sullivan would always have some control over him, having taken his heart with her when she left.

What a fool he'd been.

Chapter Thirteen

Mitch didn't need to consult the map to the McCoy estate he'd printed off the Internet to know he was approaching his destination. There was something about the high white fence and perfect spacing of the trees lining the rural road he'd taken out of colonial-looking Dependable, Missouri, that hinted at the presence of extreme wealth in the area. The white metal gate fashioned to look like the proverbial picket fence coming up on his left confirmed his suspicion.

It had seemed right to settle things first with the McCoys before he followed the other map to the address he'd found for Sullivan Investigations. He didn't have to be a genius to figure out why.

Telling his biological grandfather to get lost was far more appealing than confronting the woman who'd stolen his heart and offered up his dreams for his future as compensation to her employer. But there was no way he was going to let her off scot-free. She'd played him and deserved to be called on it.

He rolled his shoulders beneath his white shirt and tan suede blazer. He'd just prefer to do it later rather than sooner. It hurt bad enough thinking about her, let alone seeing her again.

He slowed the white sedan he'd rented at Kansas City International airport and turned onto the private drive. At the entrance, a metal column with a speaker looked as if it housed some sort of entry system, so he pulled the car close to it.

Though he'd felt sure of his course since catching the late flight out of Denver last night, he discovered his hands were damp when he released the steering wheel to lower the electric window to push a button or speak into an intercom. The rental car's blasting air conditioner kept him from being able to blame his sweaty hands on the muggy Missouri afternoon weather.

He could also easily blame his nervousness on the promissory note Donald had drafted for him to give to Joseph McCoy. The note represented the loss of everything he'd worked so hard for in the past six years. But his pride meant more to him than possessions. He technically didn't have the funds to execute the note, but Donald, in his executive capacity, had offered to guarantee the note. It was a bittersweet compliment to the quality of his operation for Donald to be so certain Mitch's herd would fetch the necessary dollar amount. Donald was also hopeful it would turn out the McCoys didn't have the right to demand the money from Mitch in the first place.

It didn't matter to Mitch. Whether it was the million bucks Marcus McCoy had paid his mom or the entire loan on his ranch, Mitch was paying some money back. He refused to be manipulated in any way, shape or form.

Before he could find a button on the column to press, a male voice came from the speaker. "Good afternoon! May I help you?"

The guy was probably a guard. A guard with very pleasant manners. Mitch glanced around until he noticed a security camera mounted on one of the gate posts. Made sense, considering the McCoys' net worth and notoriety.

Mitch leaned toward the speaker and said, "Mitch Smith here to see Joseph McCoy."

"Party prep or personal?"

"Personal." Very personal. It was his life they were messing with.

After a pause, the guy on the intercom asked, "Do you by any chance have an appointment?"

An appointment? More like a royal summons, but apparently his identity hadn't trickled down to the minions yet. "No, I don't, but I'm sure Mr. McCoy will want to see me."

"Just a moment, please."

Mitch sat back and thrummed the steering wheel with his thumb. Party prep? Then he remembered tomorrow was the Fourth of July. He dropped his head back against the seat and exhaled. The need to cut loose from the McCoys and confront Alison for what she'd done had so consumed him he'd lost track of what day it was.

"Mr. Smith," the guy on the intercom said, his tone cheerier yet. "Joseph McCoy will see you immediately."

Mitch just bet he would. McCoy was reeling him in like a gill-hooked trout. But there was no way Mitch was staying in the boat.

"Welcome to The Big House, sir." The gate silently swung open.

The Big House? Sir? Bemused, Mitch waited for the gate to clear the drive, then drove through. It was like driving onto the grounds of an exclusive country club. A single-lane road was bracketed on both sides by trees and white fences with gently rolling fields of golf-course-green grass beyond.

Then he saw the house up ahead. Okay, so it was a *Big House.* And it looked suspiciously like Thomas Jefferson's Monticello, which his family had visited when he was a kid. Only this place was bigger. A lot bigger.

The white columns and all that red brick also reminded him of many of the buildings he'd seen in Dependable on his way through town. He doubted it was a coincidence. Joseph McCoy did indeed have the power to influence and shape what he chose.

But not this cowboy.

He shouldn't have left his hat at home. Why he'd thought they'd take him more seriously without it was beyond him. He hadn't been thinking straight since Al-

ison stormed out on him. At least he'd worn his jeans
and boots with his suede blazer.

Shoving aside an ominous sinking feeling, he continued to look around as he drove slowly toward the
house. Another road, differentiated by a cobblestone
finish, branched off to the right and led to a two-story
carriage house nestled among ancient oak trees.

The closer he came to where the drive circled in front
of the impressive, double-door entry with a large half-
moon transom window above, the more vehicles he encountered, either leaving or parked off to the side of the
drive. Most were white catering vans, though there were
a couple of small box trucks.

As if paranoid he might be one of them—meaning
the McCoys or their like—despite the fact that his non-
luxury rental car was also white, the vehicles leaving all
pulled onto the grass to let him pass.

It didn't surprise him that the McCoys would want
to extravagantly celebrate the birthday of the country
that had made them so rich. Rich enough to mess with
other people's lives. Biologically connected or not, he
wanted no part of it. All he wanted was his ranch.
Whether or not he'd ever have a wife and children to
share it with was too painful for him to think about
right now.

One trial at a time.

Since the private drive ended in a paved circle bigger than the cul-de-sac on which the house he'd grown
up in had been built—along with four other houses—

he didn't have a problem finding a place to park amongst the "party prep" vehicles. After he climbed out of the car he noticed on the other side of one of the box trucks what looked like a regular driveway leading from the circle to the back of the house.

Now, the garage for a house like this might be worth seeing. He doubted Mr. McCoy would be up for a tour after Mitch told him where to stick his loan and any other potential interference he might cook up.

Mitch wanted his life back, such as it would be after he liquidated virtually everything he owned.

With his teeth clenched and all his best cuss words primed and ready to fly, Mitch strode up to the oversize white double doors. Before he could lay a knuckle to the right door he heard, "Let me, Helen," and the door was yanked open. He found himself looking just slightly down into eyes eerily similar to his own.

Behind the older man stood a slender, fifty-ish woman in a white blouse and black slacks with her hands planted on her hips and complaining in a loud whisper about not being allowed to do her job. She broke off at the sight of Mitch, her eyes going wide. Then she smiled and eased away. Probably the housekeeper.

The silver-haired man who'd opened the door, far too robust to be thought of as elderly, filled the space that the door had occupied. "Grandson."

Mitch froze. The single word was more than a greeting, more than a statement of fact.

It was an owning.

The man who could only be Joseph McCoy, billionaire and moral force to be reckoned with according to the media, was claiming Mitch. Not with arrogance and superiority, but with a love and wonder that made Mitch's anger stick in his throat.

He swallowed, forcing the anger down where he could cling to it. Mitch didn't want to be owned by anyone.

"You must be Joseph McCoy." He stuck his hand out.

Joseph took it in an equally big hand and used the opportunity to pull Mitch into an embrace with undeniable strength. "Who I am is your grandfather, and I'm well on my way to being the happiest man on God's blessed earth." His voice cracked. "You made it in time for my birthday party tonight."

His birthday party. What Alison had said came back to Mitch. Joseph had wanted his grandsons with him in time for his seventy-fifth birthday bash. And Mitch had just given him exactly what he'd wanted.

Struggling to deal with such an unexpected welcome and his disgust with himself, Mitch grunted and eased away, though he couldn't extract his hand from Joseph's iron grip, subtly or otherwise.

Joseph didn't seem to notice, let alone care. "Come in, son. Come in." He hauled Mitch into the mansion's domed, two-story foyer.

There was no sight of the woman.

Joseph finally let go of Mitch's hand to spread his hands wide. "Welcome to my home."

"The Big House," Mitch muttered, taking in dual

staircases curving upward on either side of the entry, the white-linen draped tables loaded with bright summer flowers and punch glasses lining the wide hall running beneath the stairs. A couple of weddings could take place here simultaneously, no problem.

Joseph chuckled and nodded. "Folks around here started calling it that when it was being built. Kind of stuck." He placed a hand on Mitch's shoulder and started leading him forward. "I'm so glad you arrived early enough for us to have time to talk before the party starts."

Oh, they were going to talk all right, then he was out of here for good.

"Let's go into my den where we'll have plenty of privacy." He guided Mitch to a set of double doors on the left of the hall. "Though I'm sure you're also anxious to meet your half brothers."

Mitch's heart stumbled past a couple of beats and he damn near gasped. He'd been so angry about this old guy calling in his loan and so determined to throw it right back in his face that he hadn't stopped to consider what or who else he'd encounter here in Dependable. Other than Alison, who was more than enough.

Joseph opened one of the doors and ushered Mitch in first. "Alexander is around here somewhere," he mused as he followed, closing the door behind him. "And Cooper…" He laughed, a deep rumbling noise that matched the power the man exuded despite his age. "Well, Cooper is holed up in his suite with his new fiancée, Sara Barnes. We'll give him plenty of time to make it down."

Mitch nodded but didn't process any of it. He only vaguely noted the dark wood paneling, endless shelves of books, tall multipaned windows with heavy burgundy-velvet drapes and the painted-portrait-topped fireplace.

Why had he so stubbornly ignored all the news reports and features on the revelations surrounding the "Lost Millionaires" that threatened to shake the bedrock of morality the McCoy dynasty had been built on? He would have been more prepared for what he was about to encounter.

But since there was a chance he himself would have been identified as one of those *revelations,* he hadn't wanted anything to do with the potentially torrid mess. Having certainly been filled in by their mother, his sisters had been calling him nonstop the last few days. They probably knew something about his "new" half brothers. Had he talked to Megan or Michelle, he might know what to expect from these men.

No.

He reined in his runaway thoughts to a dirt-flying halt. He was here for one thing and one thing only. To give the McCoy patriarch his promissory note, then tell him *hasta la vista,* baby. And he wouldn't be coming back.

"But before we call the others in, there's something I need to give you." Joseph strode past Mitch and went to the huge mahogany desk that dominated the room. He picked up a file thick with papers off the desk and brought it back to Mitch as if it were his first pony or something.

Mitch eyed the file folder, wary of accepting something that might tie him to this family in any way.

"Go on, take it." The sharp knowing in Joseph's eyes made Mitch realize that the success of the McCoy retail stores hadn't been accidental. The man was clearly smart as hell.

Smart enough to get Mitch to Dependable in time for the birthday party when he'd sworn not to go. Respect wiggled its way into Mitch's feelings toward Joseph, complicating matters further.

Mitch took the file folder, holding it so the papers inside didn't fall out, but he didn't open it.

Understanding softened the blue of Joseph's eyes and his slight smile deepened the groves bracketing his mouth and fanning out from his eyes. They were the lines of a man who'd smiled a lot in his life.

Mitch would, too, if he were a billionaire.

Joseph gestured to the file. "That's the deed, title, mineral rights, et cetera to the Circle S, Mitch. The place is all yours. Free and clear."

Mitch blinked, not for the first time questioning his own sanity, then frowned fiercely and flipped the folder open. As he thumbed through the loose papers within, his pulse started to pound almost as hard as when Ali son had been in the hailstorm. Sure enough, the deed to the land, the house, the loan and title papers, and other things the average Joe wouldn't be able to get his hands on, were all there.

He raised his gaze to Joseph's. "What the hell…?"

Joseph held up a staying hand. "I never wanted your money, or your ranch."

"Just the power to control me."

Joseph's eyes clouded with regret. He stepped forward and placed one of his big hands on Mitch's shoulder. "I only wanted to get a stubborn grandson here in time for my birthday party!" After giving him a squeeze and a slight shake, Joseph let go of Mitch and headed back toward the desk. Appearing very content—and why wouldn't he, having finagled getting his way—Joseph eased himself into the big leather chair behind the desk.

Mitch stared at him, shock warring with suspicion, and most powerful of all, distrust. He snapped the file folder closed and approached the desk. "Now, correct me if I have this wrong, but you bought the loan on my ranch and called it in because you knew doing so would get me here, to Dependable and The Big House, for a face-to-face."

Joseph settled his elbows on the arms of his chair and tented his fingers in front of him. "You got it."

Mitch stopped next to one of the two chairs facing the desk, tapping the corner of the folder against the armrest. "And just how, exactly, did you know I'd come?"

Joseph's smile grew wider. "Because you're a McCoy, son."

Mitch automatically rebelled against the notion. "The name doesn't make the man, sir."

"No, but what's in the blood does. And the blood in this family is strong, boy. Just look at yourself! Aside from the blond hair from your mother, you're a McCoy plain as day."

"What I am is my own man."

"I know. Miss Sullivan made that quite clear to me. Which is why I handed over the deed to your ranch."

Mitch's breathing hitched at the mention of Alison, and whatever it was that had been bedeviling him since she left squeezed his chest tight. "She told you my ranch is the most important thing to me."

Joseph raised a thick silver brow. "The most important thing?" He skewered Mitch with a doubtful look.

An image of Alison wearing too-big rain gear and jumping around in celebration among a bunch of Angus calves appeared in Mitch's mind. Then she was in his arms, smiling softly up at him....

He ruthlessly dismissed the notion that she could be anywhere near as important as his ranch and raised his chin. "With my family a close second, yes."

"Well, your family's just grown some, my boy. But as far as Miss Sullivan is concerned, all she told me during our brief conversation the day she called was that my financial obligation toward her was 'null' because she'd failed to persuade you to come here to Dependable with her. No, the ranch was entirely my idea."

Mitch's lungs went flat as if he'd been pinned against the chute by a ton of beef on the hoof. Had he misjudged Alison?

Joseph waved a hand. "Oh, she did also mention some nonsense about your 'stubborn' intent to repay that unfortunate million dollars my son paid your mother."

Spiraling toward the realization that he'd been mistaken about so many things, Mitch scrabbled to hang on to at least some of his anger as a defense. "Unfortunate because it could be construed as hush money?"

Joseph lowered his hands and sat forward, his gaze direct. "Because Marcus should have acknowledged you outright the moment he learned of your existence."

The weight of all the lies suddenly became too much to bear. "But he didn't," Mitch said flatly, and pulled the envelope containing the promissory note from his blazer's breast pocket. "So here." He stepped forward and dropped the envelope on the desk's glossy surface within Joseph's reach.

Joseph picked up the envelope and opened it. When he saw the note, he smiled smugly. "Yes, indeed, a McCoy through and through." Then he ripped the note in two.

Mitch rocked back in surprise, then recovered enough to reach out. "No—"

The halves of the note in his fists, Joseph thumped his hands down loudly on the desk. "Mitch, I don't want your money. 'Case you haven't noticed, I've got enough of my own. I only want you in my life. You're my grandson, and I want to know you. That is all. Because *my* family is the most important thing to *me*." He heaved a sigh and sat back in his big chair, for the first time looking at least a little like a man born seventy-five years ago. "Ultimately, what you do from here on out is up to you."

Mitch could only stare. This powerful man held family as dear as Mitch had been taught to. He certainly hadn't expected that.

Something shifted in Mitch. Softened. He sank into the nearest chair facing the desk, dropping the folder containing complete ownership of his life's dream in his lap.

A few minutes ago he would have sworn that dream was all that mattered to him. Now he had to admit it was a lie. Family did matter more. Sure, he'd been hurt by the secrets his mother had kept from him, but he knew from experience that he'd come to terms with what she'd done enough to forgive her.

Could he do the same with Joseph McCoy?

Mitch met Joseph's earnest gaze and the answer bloomed in his chest with healing warmth. Whether or not the man had the ability to make dreams reality, Joseph McCoy was his grandfather. The fact that Mitch was beginning to like the old guy was an added bonus.

Joseph tossed the torn and crumpled banknote and envelope onto the desk. "Though, there is the matter of the stipulations contained in my dearly departed son's last will and testament." His attention shifted to the family portrait above the fireplace.

Mitch looked there also, shocked to find so much of himself in the three people depicted in the painting.

A much younger but not much changed—aside from wavy black hair now silver and more lines on his face—

Joseph McCoy stood with his hand on the shoulder of a seated beautiful, elegant woman. She had equally black hair with thick curls and kind blue eyes.

The need to know stirred. "Your wife?"

"Your grandmother. Elise. God rest her soul."

True regret settled in Mitch's chest. "I'm sorry, sir."

Joseph nodded. "So am I."

Mitch studied the portrait again, allowing his gaze to touch on the author of so much turmoil. Next to his grandmother stood a boy sporting a bit of a smirk that Mitch found disturbingly familiar. But the smirk had nothing on the eyes. The man that kid had grown into was definitely his father.

A surreal feeling overcame Mitch. A magnification of how he'd felt when he'd learned what he'd thought was the truth of his paternity the first time. Instead of finding out what he *wasn't,* he was discovering what he *was.* A McCoy.

Trying to refocus on the conversation, he said, "The stipulations requiring me to take my rightful place in the family and company."

Joseph blinked the moisture from his eyes and sniffed loudly. "Yes."

It hit Mitch that it hadn't been all that long since this man had buried his son. Mitch's father. Sympathy for Joseph stirred, but Mitch couldn't personally grieve for someone who'd caused so much difficulty. "I'm sorry for your loss, sir."

"It would do this battered old heart of mine a world

of good to hear you call me Grandpa. Or Grandfather, if you prefer."

Mitch rolled the idea around in his head. There wasn't much point in fighting the fact that he was bound to Joseph, even if he still wanted to. He didn't. The realization felt like having a dead steer lifted off his chest. For the first time in weeks he felt liberated.

And he wanted to grant his grandfather's wish. But he'd make the familiarity his own. "I'm sorry, Grandpa Joe."

Joseph McCoy, one of the richest men in the nation, misted up like Mabel always did when one of her grandkids came into her store bearing a fistful of wildflowers. "Thank you, Mitch. I'd say that amounts to taking your rightful place in this family."

His chest full and his throat suspiciously tight in response to Joseph's emotions, Mitch dropped his gaze to his never-quite-clean-looking hands. They were the hands of a hardworking man.

The man he was proud to be.

He didn't belong in a place like this. "Will or no, my life is on my ranch. That's my dream. Always has been, always will be."

"I understand having a dream." Joseph tented his fingers again. "And I've been thinking it might be time for McCoy Enterprises to diversify a bit." He cocked a brow. "Perhaps into the beef industry. Would you be interested in a silent—and I mean *very* silent—partner, Mitch?"

Considering why he'd come here, it was no big surprise that his knee-jerk reaction was to say *hell, no.* He tempered it by saying, "I don't know, sir—"

"You have my word you'll have complete autonomy."

Mitch mulled the offer over, turning the file folder on his lap. Maybe it would be better to be part of this family on his own terms. And somewhere along the way, Joseph had ceased to be the enemy. "I guess it's worth considering."

His grandfather tapped his fingertips together, looking very pleased. "That way you'd be a part—a wholly independent part, as I promised—of the family business, taking care of the final stipulation. What do you think?"

"I think I could live with that."

"Excellent." Joseph stood and offered Mitch his hand across the expanse of desk.

Mitch grabbed the folder off his lap and stood, also. He shook his grandfather's hand. The connection was warm. Solid. "I have to say, this is not how I expected today to go at all." Nothing like an old guy tearing up over your mere presence to take the fight out of you.

Joseph squeezed Mitch's hand. "Embrace the unexpected and make it work for you, my boy."

As if on cue, a knock sounded at the door.

In his exuberance, Joseph released Mitch's hand and good-naturedly bellowed, "Come in!"

The door opened and Mitch gaped as a black-haired version of himself walked in. "Helen banged on my

door and…told me…I might want to get down here…."
The man, roughly Mitch's age, gaped right back.

"Cooper!" Joseph rounded the desk and headed for the new arrival with an arm extended. "I have someone special for you to meet."

Cooper snapped his mouth shut, then raised a dark brow. "Let me guess, another Lost Millionaire has found his way home."

Joseph snorted, but his smile was still wide as he drew Cooper farther into the den. "More like dragged kicking and screaming."

"Him, too?" Cooper locked gazes with Mitch, his blue eyes assessing but sparking with humor. "Cool. We'll get along just fine." He extended a hand. "Cooper Anders. Call me Coop."

Mitch took his hand and shook it, feeling the oddest connection with the guy. Maybe it was his imagination. Or maybe being raised with only sisters had made him unwittingly hungry for a brotherly kinship.

Coop gave one last squeeze. "Don't worry, being part of this family will take some getting used to, but you'll get there."

Because it came from similar experience, Mitch appreciated his understanding.

Joseph asked, "Where's that lovely lady of yours, Cooper?"

Cooper coughed behind his fist, but couldn't quite seem to contain a grin. "She's…um…getting her act together."

Joseph sent Cooper a slightly censoring look, but his obvious pleasure couldn't be contained, either. "My VP of Operations never had to 'get her act together' before you came along, young man."

Cooper shrugged. "Guess it's hereditary."

That earned him a smack on his broad shoulder from his grandfather. Their grandfather. Mitch wished again that he'd worn his hat—so he could hang on to the brim to keep his head from spinning so much. He had to settle for holding the file folder tight in his hands.

The door to the den opened again and yet another dark-haired version of himself walked in. Only this one was a few years older with circles under his blue eyes and a harder line to his mouth. "Helen said you wanted to see me." His gaze skipped from Joseph to Cooper, then landed on Mitch. He froze. "Oh."

Joseph went to the new arrival as if he might have to keep him from bolting back out of the room. "Our cowboy from Colorado has arrived. Now all we're missing is our marine. Come meet Mitch Smith, your and Cooper's half brother."

Though he didn't know why, Mitch felt the need to be the one to go shake this half brother's hand. There was a bruised wariness in his eyes that made Mitch want to take care with him.

Mitch freed a hand and reached it out to him. "Rancher, actually, from Whiskey Ridge."

They shook hands, and again he felt that weird connection. It had to be from their physical similarities. All three of them were roughly the same height and build, though these two's bulk looked more of the gym-acquired sort.

"Alexander McCoy," the newest arrival said in an automatic way as he obviously took stock of Mitch.

"It's nice to meet you." Mitch did some stock-taking of his own. Alexander was different, somehow. He carried a burden they didn't.

Beaming like nobody's business, Joseph said, "You two will have plenty to talk about. I know you're a cattleman, Mitch, but I'm sure you have a horse or two at your place, right?"

"Twelve, actually."

Joseph clapped them both on the shoulder. "Marvelous! Alexander, here, raises racehorses in his spare time, such as it is, right out back." To Alexander he said, "Why don't you take Mitch to see your stable?"

A muscle worked in Alexander's jaw as he looked at Joseph. Clearly he wasn't game for playing meet-the-family at the moment. "I'm afraid there are a few things still to see to for your party tonight." He shifted his gaze to Mitch. "Perhaps another time."

Though he planned to be heading back home as soon as possible, Mitch nodded. "Sure."

To Joseph, Alexander said, "I do need to speak with you right now, though."

"Regarding what?"

Alexander glanced at Mitch and Cooper behind him,

the wariness in his eyes now tinged with frustration. "Regarding that reporter you've invited to cover the party tonight."

Joseph pulled back his chin. "Maddy Monroe? What about her?"

"She's still insisting on interviews."

That seemed to get Joseph's interest, and it was his turn to glance at Mitch and Cooper. "Will you excuse us just a moment, boys?"

Mitch said, "Sure."

Coop added, "No problem."

Joseph snagged Alexander's elbow and led him away a step or two. Mitch backed up to stand next to Cooper, who was watching the other two men closely.

Then something occurred to Mitch. He softly wondered, "Alexander *McCoy?*"

Cooper leaned toward him. "Your ranch must be out in the middle of nowhere. Alexander was dear old Daddy's first bouncing-baby near-scandal. Helen, the housekeeper—" He held up a hand. "Don't ask. It'll take longer than I've got now to explain. Buy me a beer later at The Office and I'll give you the complete scoop.

"But anyway, the housekeeper is Alex's mom. Grandpap and Grandma—" he gestured toward the portrait "—decided it would be better if they passed him off as theirs. Alex found out the same time they found out about us that he's his brother's son." Cooper frowned as if he was momentarily as confused as Mitch.

Cooper's brow cleared. "Yes, that's right. Needless to say it hasn't sat well, finding out things aren't how he thought."

Stunned, Mitch looked at Alexander in a new light. It appeared he and his oldest half brother had more in common than just horses. But finding out Ed Smith wasn't really his father was nowhere near as shocking as what Alexander had had to face. Mitch returned his attention to the boy in the painted portrait. "So many lies generated from one person's actions."

Cooper scoffed. "He was hound dog through and through."

Remembering Alison's comment about Mitch's hound dog behavior, he blanched.

He went back to watching the two men talking. Now he knew why Alexander seemed so different. He'd been raised here, and while his life would change the least because of Marcus McCoy's will, his perception of himself might change the most.

Tapping the file folder against his leg, Mitch mused, "It'll be a wonder if any of us will ever be able to trust again." He immediately thought of Alison, and his guts twisted. Had she really had nothing to do with Joseph deciding to go after the Circle S? Could he hang on to his anger if she had?

"Won't know till you try, brother. Worked for me. Hell, I found love in the enemy's camp, so I highly recommend giving it a shot."

Mitch thought of the directions to Sullivan Investigations on the dash of his rental car. Did he dare go to see her with the intent of trusting her instead of confronting her?

The need to see her, regardless of what he decided to do, seized him with the same power as the hail storm that had brought them closer.

Alexander and Joseph seemed to come to an agreement on the matter of the reporter, and Alexander stepped toward the door.

He raised a hand to Mitch. "I have to go, but welcome to the family."

Mitch pulled at the brim of an imaginary hat in return and watched Alexander leave.

It was time for Mitch to do the same. He didn't want to wait a moment longer to track down Alison.

When Joseph rejoined him and Cooper, Mitch said, "I have to go, too."

Joseph's gray brows slammed together. "Go? But you just arrived!"

"I'll be back, I swear. In time for the party." If he was going to accept his connection to the McCoys, he might as well go all the way.

"What do you need to do? I have people here more than willing to—"

"No, really," Mitch stopped him. "This is something I have to do myself." He glanced at Cooper. "A trust I have to try to re-earn."

Cooper raised his brows, then grinned in understanding. "Won't know till you try."

Joseph pinned Mitch with an intense, I'm-the-boss look. "But you'll be back by this evening."

Touched by his grandfather's need for his presence, Mitch answered solemnly. "Yes, sir. Promise."

Joseph visibly relaxed. "Then go."

Mitch nodded a goodbye at them both and strode to the door.

Before he was through it, Joseph called, "And give Miss Sullivan my eternal thanks."

Mitch faltered and looked back. Joseph's smile was smug, and Cooper was rolling his eyes at their grandfather's intuitiveness.

The sort of happiness Mitch had experienced only with his mom, Ed and his sisters swelled in him. Okay, so he did have room in his life for more family.

But he still needed to see a pretty lady about his heart.

Chapter Fourteen

Mitch turned his rental car from Dependable's two-lane Main Street into the parking lot of a brick-faced, U-shaped business park bearing the address he was looking for.

Compared to quaint little Whiskey Ridge with its whopping three hundred people spread out over miles, Dependable, Missouri, was a bustling metropolis. The sign coming into town had claimed ten thousand people were proud to call Dependable their home, and from what he'd seen, with good reason.

He scanned the large tinted windows and glass doors on the single-story buildings until he spotted Sullivan Investigations in gold letters on one of the doors, though the words were partially obscured by a piece of paper taped there. He parked in one of several empty spaces directly in front of the door and climbed out of the car.

Business wasn't exactly hopping. And Alison had released Joseph of any "financial obligation" because she'd failed to gain Mitch's cooperation.

His conscience, on the rampage since Joseph had cleared Alison of being responsible for the loan call-in, gave him a good swift kick.

Man, he was getting good at being a fool.

Mitch grabbed the door handle, but before he yanked it open, what turned out to be an official notice taped to the glass door caught his attention.

A Notice of Foreclosure.

His mouth went dry and his heart pounded in his ears. He read on. There was a bankruptcy hearing pending involving Sullivan Investigations. Any and all creditors were to contact the court.

He remembered thinking that they all had a sad story of some kind. He officially made the move from fool to ass.

If only she'd accepted his offer of help.

But if she had, would he care about her as much? And exactly how much was that?

Judging by the fact that he hadn't been able to stop thinking about her, by how much it had hurt when she'd left, by how eviscerating her "betrayal" had been and how relieved he'd felt to discover she was innocent, he cared for her a lot.

A hell of a lot.

Dammit, he'd gone and fallen in love with her. Every stubborn, independent inch of her.

And she probably hated his guts.

Mitch jerked open the door and went in. He stepped into a small reception area. A lone office was situated behind a partially closed door to the right. A door to a rest room was on the left.

The reception area looked like a million other reception areas for a million other small businesses. A few black chairs that stopped being comfortable five minutes into a twenty-minute wait. A fake tree in the corner collecting dust. A half counter with a Please Ring Bell for Service sign next to the required bell and a desk on the other side of the counter for the receptionist.

The receptionist who'd run off to Mexico with her married boss.

Mitch's stomach turned and his fist itched for contact with a certain previously married boss's face.

A drawer slammed in the office. Mitch quietly stepped over to the oak door that had once sported a nameplate that had been pried off, judging by the marks in the wood. *Atta girl,* he thought with grim satisfaction. She really was something.

His body added a *damn straight* when he spotted Alison bending over one of several boxes consuming the floor space in the small office. Her khaki pants molded to her shapely bottom, but had nothing on the black jeans she'd worn in Colorado.

Then he noticed the makeshift, though tidy, bed.

His jaw clenched tight. Unless she was housing some unseen transient, Alison had been sleeping in a green quilted sleeping bag on a folding cot in her ex-husband's office. This time not only did his stomach turn and his fist itch, but his blood boiled.

He unclenched his jaw enough to say, "You really should keep that outer door locked."

Alison lurched upright and turned, launching the paper contents of a file into the air in the process. If he wasn't so crapped off about her situation it would have been funny. Paper floated down and caught on her dark blue blouse and in her long red curls.

Recognition eased her startled expression and she put a hand over her heart. "Jeez, Mitch, you scared me." Her eyes went wide again. "Mitch! What are you doing here?"

He pushed a box aside with the toe of his boot and came farther into the office. "Had some business to attend to."

Her expression shuttered. "Oh." She squatted to retrieve the papers that had fluttered to the ground next to the box. "It's business hours for me, too. If I locked the outer doors, clients wouldn't be able to get in."

Pleased for her sake, he asked, "You have clients?"

She paused in the act of placing a document back in the file folder. "Potential clients."

"Ah." The foreboding returned. He gestured to the cot, the sleeping bag folded down at the top to reveal its blue plaid interior, the white pillow placed on top. "You going for the 'work is my life' look?"

She snapped the file closed and dropped it in the box. "It's either that or live in my car. Which, actually, I'll be doing in a week unless I land some work."

The defeat in her tone tore at his insides. If it weren't for the boxes in his way, he would have gone to her, gathered her in his arms and never let go. Then again, it was probably better to go slowly.

"Will you miss this?" He waved an encompassing hand at the office.

Long auburn curls danced as she shook her head. "No. This was Scott's dream. I tried to make a go of it because he told me I wouldn't be able to do the job, that I'd fail." She stared at the disarray for a moment, then gave a harsh snort. "Turned out he was right."

Mitch's throat closed up on him, hating what she was going through. She looked so defeated, so *wrong*. He never wanted his brave, determined Alison to look that way again.

Before he could say as much, she stood and planted her hands on her hips. A challenging light sparked in her eyes. "I figured you'd just mail the check to the McCoys."

Hallelujah. She wasn't broken, after all. His heart swelled up with so much love for her it was a wonder his shirt buttons didn't pop off. He rubbed a hand over his jaw until he'd conquered the urge to grin like a goof. He'd end up with a boot print on his rump if she thought he was laughing at her. Assuming she was wearing her boots.

He shifted so he could see her feet. Sensible loafers. She really was in a bad way.

He crossed his arms over his chest, the suede blazer binding over his shoulders. "Why so sure I was able to come up with the money?"

She rolled her eyes and returned to her packing. She grabbed a stack of file folders off the desk. "Because you're the type of guy who can do anything you set your mind to, Mitch."

Even get the girl? He bit his tongue. He needed to apologize first. But her praise and confidence in him made him want to crow.

When he remained silent, her movements became jerky, as if she felt self-conscious or unsure. "So, what do you think of Dependable?"

"It's nice. And I saw firsthand that you weren't lying about or exaggerating Grandpa Joe's generosity. If the number of buildings with his name on them is any indication, he's been spreading at least some of that fortune of his around."

She stilled, but didn't look at him. "Grandpa Joe?"

"Yeah. The old guy isn't so bad. Even though he did tear up my promissory note."

When she met his gaze, the hope in her eyes made his throat burn. "So you've accepted being a McCoy?"

"I'm striving to 'embrace the unexpected and make it work for me.'" He shrugged. "But I haven't stopped believing that the name doesn't make the man. I'm still my own man." The urge to grin finally won out. "Who just happens to now own his ranch free and clear."

She scrunched her auburn brows together. "But your mortgage…?"

Her confusion would have been enough to dismiss any doubts if he'd had them about her knowledge of Joseph's scheme to haul him here through his loan.

Mitch eased his way around the boxes toward her as he explained. "After you quit and took off—"

She looked away and a flush crept up her throat as she worked to swallow. It must have been awful for her to accept defeat that way, to think her rotten ex had been right.

Mitch couldn't help but soften his tone "—I was notified that the loan on my ranch had not only been bought, but was being called in."

Her gaze jerked back to his. *"What?"*

The obvious outrage on his behalf warmed him to his soul. "Joseph had bought my mortgage and was demanding payment."

Her brows came together again. "Why in the world would he want—"

"He knew it would get me here. He was right."

She chewed on that for a moment, her eyes narrowing. "He baited you into coming."

"Apparently my pride is hereditary."

"And you've forgiven him for it?"

He nodded, stopping right in front of her and losing himself in the tangle of blues and greens of her eyes. "Kinda hard not to. Turns out the old guy just wanted a chance to hug his 'new' grandson."

She blinked up at him. "You really believe that?"

There was that trust thing again. He reached up and brushed a curl away from her face. She was so beautiful and caring. "Yeah, I actually do. Especially after he found a pretty simple way for me to satisfy the stipulations of the will without having to change my life much at all."

"You don't have to join their family business?"

"Their family business is joining mine."

Her brows went up.

He grinned. "Joseph has asked if he can invest in my ranch. Seems he's had a sudden urge to diversify."

"You're not afraid of him having power over you?"

This time Mitch brushed his fingers across her smooth jaw. "The only one who could ever have power over me is you, Alison."

Alison's heart jolted against her ribs so hard she swayed toward the incredible man standing before her.

She was dreaming. The cowboy she'd been fantasizing about coming to save her from the nightmare of her failure really wasn't standing here. His tantalizingly rough fingertips on her face weren't raising goose bumps all over her body. His velvety words weren't raising her hopes for something she'd thought would never be....

Apparently she still affected him, only this time he didn't sound unhappy about it. Just the opposite.

"Oh, my." She swayed again.

He grabbed hold of her waist and steadied her. "Alison? Are you okay?"

She could feel the warmth and strength of his hands through her blouse. Two things she was so in need of now. She rested her own hands on his forearms. The soft suede of his jacket a nice compliment to the hardness beneath. "I'm fine. It's just a little much to take in."

"You haven't eaten lately, have you?"

She laughed wryly. "I can't seem to take care of myself in all sorts of ways."

He squeezed her waist gently. "That's not true. So many things have been taken out of your control. You can't blame yourself."

"Sure I can. I vowed to make it on my own, Mitch, but all I've wanted since I came back was for you to come rescue me from myself. I'm too stinking stubborn to accept my parents' offer to move back with them, even though I've never been so lonely and unhappy in all my life."

Mitch crushed her to him, sliding his hands from her waist to completely surround her with his strength. He rested his cheek against her hair.

Exactly what she needed. She brought her arms up around his neck and held on tight.

His heart pounded against her breast. "Oh, Alison. It kills me that you're feeling this way when you're so courageous and so capable. I admire and love you so much."

Every cell in Alison stilled. How she wanted to believe—

He held her tighter yet. If she had been breathing, it would have become difficult.

A grumbling sound vibrated deep in his broad chest. "You don't have to be alone to be independent. I know I screwed up bad with you, but I swear, if you agree to come home with me, you'll truly be my partner—not some sort of foreman—in life *and* on the ranch."

He pulled back to look at her. "Please say you can forgive me enough to at least think about it?"

Certain lack of oxygen had affected her hearing, Alison pushed away from him. Worry mingled with the love and desperation in his blue eyes, but he loosened his hold enough on her so she could take a step back.

She had to be sure this time. She'd made so many faulty assumptions about what Scott had been offering her, what he wanted from her.

She looked him square in the eye. "What are you asking of me, Mitch?"

"I'm asking for your forgiveness."

"I got that part." Her heart was racing so fast it made her light-headed. "But you said…you said you loved… me…."

His eyes shimmering, he reached out and cupped her face with his hands. "I do, Alison. I've fallen in love with you. I couldn't help it."

Her own vision blurry, she half laughed, half cried at his declaration. "I'm sorry."

He shook his head, his expression serious. "I'm not. And I'm asking you to spend your life with me."

Hope and wonder almost knocked her flat. There was no stopping the tears now. "You are?"

His beautiful smile was so loving and understanding and his touch so tender on her cheeks. "If you can forgive me enough to consider it. I also promise you'll get a good dose of town life when we come back here to visit. As often as you like. Though I have a sneaking suspicion Joseph will develop the occasional need for dry, Colorado air."

Love exploded in her and propelled her into his arms again. "Oh, Mitch, I can do more than forgive you. I'm making a new vow to love and cherish you, with every stubborn, determined inch of me, for the rest of my life."

She stroked his thick, wavy hair. "And I don't care if you're a Smith or a McCoy, only that you'll forever be my cowboy."

He looked her deep in the eye, radiating more love than she'd thought possible. "That I can do, sweetheart." His grinned widened. "That I can do."

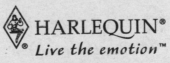

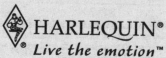

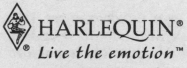

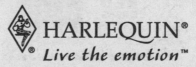

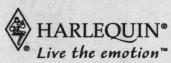